Nico Hamurişi is the one and only son of Santa Claus. All his life, Nico has known he's expected to fall in love and find lifelong commitment by the Christmas of his thirtieth year—like every other heir before him. But knowing and accepting are vastly different things, and as the final countdown begins, Nico has yet to embrace his fate. His once great enthusiasm for eventually becoming Santa has been dimmed by uncertainty over how the Santa Line will be affected when he marries a man.

With only a year left, will Nico have time to find love and commitment all while learning how magic will transform the family line to accommodate who he is and who he loves?

LOVE BLOOMS

Stephanie Hoyt

A NineStar Press Publication

Published by NineStar Press
P.O. Box 91792,
Albuquerque, New Mexico, 87199 USA.
www.ninestarpress.com

Love Blooms

Printed in the USA
First Edition
December, 2018

Print ISBN: 978-1-949909-66-1

Also available in eBook, ISBN: 978-1-949909-60-9

Warning: This book contains sexually explicit content, which may only be suitable for mature readers.

To Kenny and Kimothy, my forever cheerleaders

Chapter One

THE SUN HASN'T even begun to brighten the sky when Nico reaches the family estate. He shuts his car's engine off in front of his childhood home and waits, staring at his watch as the seconds tick by. The hour hand strikes five and snow starts to fall. His father must have made his first delivery right on time. Nico sighs, relief washing over him at having successfully avoided the annual Christmas conversation for the next twenty-something hours. For the moment, no matter how fleeting, he can go inside without bracing himself for confrontation.

The snow falls soft and cold on his face as he walks to the door, and for an instant, Nico thinks it may have been worth coming home earlier to avoid the snowfall. He laughs, short and bitter, as last year's predelivery family dinner flashes in his mind and he remembers what avoiding the snowfall entails. He'd much rather deal with this cold, wet mess than the disappointment in his father's eyes at another year passing by without him fulfilling his obligations as heir apparent. If last year was bad, this year will be infinitely worse. His father had been disappointed then, but now with the deadline looming so close, Nico can imagine how his father's mood will have shifted to something far worse than disappointment.

He wipes his feet on the welcome home mat and opens the door. He takes a deep breath as he steps inside and tries his best not to let this place get the better of him. It stopped being home years ago, but he can do this. He can. Except, the utter lack of even a shred of welcoming quality fills him with dread. This house has been the site of nearly every argument he's ever had with his father and he knows he's opened the door to yet another lecture on the expectations and obligations that come along with being the son of Kristoff Hamurişi.

This year won't be any different, especially since the final year of the countdown begins at midnight. If he's being realistic, which he hates to do, any discussion of his failings is going to be much more tense than they've ever been before. But for now, the lights inside are off, save for the Christmas tree, his father is out for more than a full day's worth of deliveries, the rest of the house seems to be fast asleep, and Nico can slip upstairs to his childhood bedroom without being noticed.

At least, that's what he was counting on.

Unfortunately for him, someone had different plans for his arrival. He opens his bedroom door to a lit room and a ball of limbs and hair curled up in the middle of his bed. He sets his suitcase down with a loud thud and the ball moves, revealing the face of Noelle, the youngest of his four older sisters.

"My dear little Santicholas," she says, words and laughter both swallowed in a yawn. "I can't believe you thought you could sneak in here unnoticed."

Nico rolls his eyes. "You know I hate when you call me that."

She untangles herself and pushes up on the tips of her toes to wrap her arms around Nico in a big, tight hug. "It's hard to believe you do when you're smiling so big."

Nico's words get muffled by her hair and his own laughter. "Yeah, yeah. I missed you, too."

She lets him go, shaking her head as he starts to yawn. "You should've come home at a decent hour if you wanted to be well rested."

Nico narrows his eyes. "If it's such an indecent hour then why are you up?"

Noelle lets out a short huff of air, annoyed. "I wanted you to see a friendly face before..."

Nico closes his eyes. *Here it comes.* He should have known better than to think he could avoid confrontation, even for a moment, even from his closest friend and sibling. When he opens his eyes again, Noelle's sitting on the edge of the bed and her face has softened in a way that makes Nico feel worse.

He smiles but it does nothing to wipe the gentle expression off her face; she knows him too well, knows he wears it as a shield.

"You don't have to pretend with me. I know failing is what worries you."

"Failure isn't my concern here, Noelle." *Not entirely true.* "I'm worried about what will happen if I *don't* fail." *Unbearably true.*

Noelle raises her eyebrow, confused, and Nico's stomach clenches. *Am I actually doing this?* He plows on before she can interrupt and he loses his nerve. "And I'm angry! I'm so incredibly angry I even need to be concerned by all this shit in the first place. I don't want to think of heirs and continuing a family legacy and everything else riding on me falling in love when I don't even know how *who* I love will affect any of this."

Noelle blinks, breathing out a barely audible "Oh."

Nico's heart skips, his pulse is erratic.

"I'm gay."

Noelle blinks again, and again, and again, and then, after what feels like an eternity of his stomach turning over in knots, she smiles. "Okay."

"Okay?"

"Yes, okay."

She motions for Nico to sit next to her, and he does, knocking his shoulder against hers. "I was expecting a little more than an okay, if I'm being honest."

Noelle laughs, embarrassed. "I didn't think I should start quizzing you on if you're seeing anyone, so okay seemed, well...okay."

Nico smiles, and this time it's not a shield. He feels lighter and more at peace in this house than he has in years. It's such a relief to have finally shared such an important part of himself with such an important person in his life.

"Who all knows?"

Nico doesn't answer immediately, and Noelle asks, "Oh, am I the only one who knows?"

"No, it's not exactly a secret. I mean, everyone I know who doesn't know this family knows. So work and friends from college and yeah. I'm basically out to everyone except the family."

Noelle appears confused and curious. "Not even Joy? She knows how—"

Nico cuts her off. "No, not even our dear lesbian sister knows. Only you."

Noelle hums an acknowledgment but doesn't say anything else for a long while—Nico can tell she's working through what to say next.

He has an idea of what she might be thinking and supplies an answer, "I haven't told Mom and Dad because, even though it wasn't a thing when Joy came out, what if... I mean it's got to be different when you don't have to produce an heir."

Nico can't keep the disdain out of his voice. For as long as he can remember, the heir has been his biggest concern regarding his father and, in turn, his mother finding out his sexuality. "There's all this added pressure surrounding me finding someone to love. I know they don't have a problem with queer people, but what if they have a problem with *me* being gay. There's a lot riding on my love life."

"Okay," Noelle nods. "Well, yeah. I can't deny there is a lot of pressure put on you falling in love. But I've got your back here. No matter what happens, I'll help you find out how this affects you being the heir apparent to the Crimson Sleigh."

Nico bursts out in laughter. "God, shut up. Why do you insist on calling it that?"

Noelle smiles, pleased as can be. "Because it makes you laugh."

Nico purses his lips, trying to stifle his laughter. "You're ridiculous, you know?"

"Yes, obviously. But I am also wonderful and magical and dearly beloved by you."

"I guess." He draws the word out, teasing, and Noelle shoves him, laughing. "Though I wouldn't consider magical one of your finer qualities since we all are."

Noelle crinkles her nose. "If you got it, flaunt it."

Nico sighs. He wishes he was pleased with the extra magic they have, but it's different—like everything else— when the full extent of his own powers is contingent on falling in love. "I'd much rather have no magic at all, but that's probably just me."

"Yeah, it's got to be just you." She pauses, furrowing her brow in thought. "Is it even possible to have no magic, though? Everyone's got some when it comes down to it, even the Immunes. Magic's everywhere little bro; it's a fact of life."

"I'd gladly trade with anyone who doesn't have a love stipulation placed on their magic." He doesn't mean to sound so wishful, but so much of his life since college has been spent wondering how his life would be if he didn't have all this extra pressure resting on his shoulders. He'd much rather be gifted with any other sort of magic; no need for the frills of Santahood. "Besides, I'm not much more powerful than anyone but Dad as it is. Since love eludes me."

Noelle's eyes light up. "So you're *not* seeing anyone?"

Nico shakes his head, chuckling. He can always count on Noelle for poor segues and making him laugh. "Have you been waiting this whole time to ask me?"

"No, of course not; that'd be absurd. But since you've brought it back up..."

"I didn't exactly bring it up."

Noelle waves her hand, dismissing his words. "Yeah, yeah. But you gave me the perfect opportunity to ask, so."

"So, what?" Nico knows what she means, but he wants to mess with her, make her work for the answer.

"So"—she draws the word out, her warm brown eyes twinkling with familiar mirth—"are you or are you not seeing anyone?"

"No, not at the moment."

Noelle seems surprised, and Nico supplies an answer before she can ask, "It's not necessarily a coincidence I pursued a career in something that affords me the opportunity to travel so much—I'm not entirely sure I want to settle down or fall in love."

It's the unfortunate truth of his life, but Noelle's face falls. She isn't pleased with the answer.

"Oh, Nico. You can't deny yourself love because of the things expected of you. That's not fair to yourself."

Nico shrugs. He wishes it were that simple, but his obligations are always at the back of his mind, and it only gets worse when he meets a man who has the potential to be something more. Noelle smiles, soft and sympathetic. She gets up and ruffles his hair like she has since they were children; her fingers catch at the end where it's starting to curl, and she clucks her tongue. It's annoying and comforting all at the same time, as it always has been, and more of Nico's tension slips away. Noelle's always been such a good friend. "Mom will be up soon enough, and the rest of the house won't be much longer after that."

Nico yawns and Noelle continues, hand on the door, ready to leave, "The kids missed you last night so you might want to nap and get a story ready for why you didn't arrive with everyone else because I'm sure they'll pester you for one. Especially Timmy. Belle says he's become quite the inquisitive little boy as of late."

Nico motions for the door. "Will you stop fretting over me and go already. You said I need a nap. So let me nap."

"Okay, okay. I'm going," she says, but before she closes the door, she peeks her head back through and says, "I'm going to help you figure this all out, Nico. I promise."

She shuts the door and Nico, for the first time in a long time, feels calm and relieved and a tad hopeful since he's told Noelle. She's right: he shouldn't deny himself love. There might be a deadline and a world of responsibilities, obligations, and powers that come with being the heir apparent to the sleigh, but at the very least, he can't let this change what he wants. He can't let a part of his life he has never had a say in control his happiness.

He wants to fall in love; he wants to settle down; he wants to open his heart and build a life with someone else. And honestly, Nico thinks, as he starts to doze off, Santa be damned if being gay will change any of that.

Chapter Two

NICO WAKES UP three hours later to a loud knock at his door. He's groggy and a little disoriented, and he wishes he had come home this afternoon, instead of trying to avoid everyone by getting in before dawn. He wasn't successful, anyway; all he managed to do was avoid his father.

"Come in," Nico calls through a yawn. He's expecting to see one or more of his sisters' children come through the door. Instead, his mother, Gloria, walks through the door with a big, kind smile and a mug in hand. Her long gray hair is perfectly styled and her warm brown skin is glowing in the morning light, and Nico's stomach, for a moment, curls in shame over still being in bed.

"Good morning, Nicholas. I brought you a cup of coffee with an absurd amount of sugar—exactly how you like."

She sets it on his nightstand, and he mutters his thanks. She nudges him to sit up and scoot over so she can sit with him at the edge of the bed. He obliges and she continues talking as he begins to drink, "We missed you last night."

"Mhm." Nico hums into his coffee mug. He knew skipping the predelivery dinner would upset his mother the most, and at the time, he thought it'd be worth it, but really it just stings hearing the disappointment in her voice.

"Sorry," he mumbles, all the calmness that washed over him after talking to Noelle is gone now. Instead, he's left with clammy hands and a nervous heartbeat. His mother looks at him as if she expects greatness, and it instantly takes him back to being a child searching for approval.

"I shouldn't have flaked. I'm sorry, I—"

"Didn't want to be here?"

Nico would feel much worse she knows the truth if it weren't for the faintest hint of a smile on her face—she seems to understand. "You know me too well, Mom."

Her smile grows and the guilt in the pit of his stomach begins to shrink. "You can't hide things from me. I'm very perceptive."

"Yeah, you are," he says, while thinking *if only you knew.*

"Oh?" She raises an eyebrow. "You doubt me?"

Nico laughs. "No, of course I don't. You *are* very perceptive but—"

"But you're hiding something else," she supplies.

Nico blinks and his chest aches with nerves. "What?"

"It doesn't take your kind of magic, or any for that matter, to figure out there's a reason you hate—"

"I don't—"

"There's no need to lie. I may not be as intuitive as you or your father, but I know my own children. And I know there is something more to your avoidance of this family and this house and this deadline than you want to let on. There's something more to you no longer wanting to be Santa Claus."

"That's true."

Gloria appears surprised he admitted it, but Nico knows there's no use in fumbling out a denial. Not with her. Not anymore. He doesn't want to be Santa, he hasn't for a long time, not if the process and his duties after he takes over are complicated, or made impossible, by who he is. By who he's attracted to. "There's actually something I need to tell you. And Dad..."

He trails off. It's harder to tell his mom than Noelle. Noelle has always been in his corner, and while his mother has, too, it's in a much different way.

Gloria doesn't push Nico when it becomes apparent he has no intention of finishing his thought. Instead, she pats the side of his face with her hand. It's a familiar gesture—something she used to do when he was having a bad day—but startling all the same. It's been so long since he's allowed himself to be vulnerable in front of her, or anyone, that he's not expecting it at all. He takes a long drink of his coffee to soothe the ache creeping into the back of his throat. His mother smiles, a small, sad little thing, and the knot in his throat grows. "Nico, whatever it is—whatever is holding you back and making you not want this life anymore—we can get through it. Together. As a family. All you have to do is tell us."

There are so many things he wants to say. So many questions he needs to ask. So many answers she won't have. So many things only his father will know, but all of it is far easier said than done.

"I..." He's a fish out of water. He doesn't know how to form his thoughts into coherent sentences. He shakes his head. "There's something big I've been meaning to tell you and Dad and everyone."

Gloria's eyes widen, a hopeful smile curling the edge of her lips, and Nico's stomach drops. "No, I haven't met anyone."

She does her best not to show her disappointment, but Nico can tell she is, anyway. "I still have time." It's as much an affirmation for himself as it is for her.

"I know you do." She seems much more sure of it than he does. "You're a wonderfully kind and charming man and quite handsome at that. Any woman would be lucky to have you."

And there it is: the gut-wrenching assumption that's plagued him for so long.

"Mom, please."

"Don't be embarrassed, hon."

"I'm not." Which is true. But he doesn't have any time to counter her point any further before his door flies open with a raucous burst of laughter. In stumbles Timmy and Annette, with Max toddling not too far behind them.

"Uncle Nico!" Timmy shouts, beaming. "Where were you last night?"

Gloria glances toward Nico as Timmy reaches out for him. He pushes out of bed, finally, and scoops Timmy up in a hug. "I was finishing up some last minute work before Christmas."

He feels guilty for lying, but he can't tell his five-year-old nephew the truth. His mother purses her lips but doesn't acknowledge the blatant lie, and Timmy is none the wiser. Annette turns her attention to Nico, one hand clasped around Max's hand, the other on her hip. Her similarity to an impatient Carol is uncanny, and Nico laughs, "You look exactly like your Mom."

He sets Timmy down and picks Annette up, reaching down with the other hand to ruffle Max's hair. "Little man, you're getting so big."

He smiles painfully wide and Annette adds, "I can't even carry him anymore!"

She sounds so excited, which is where she deviates from her mother. Carol always complained as he and Noelle grew. She hated not being able to carry them around anymore.

"Come on, little ones. Let's go round up the rest of the kids. I have someplace special to show you."

Gloria gives him a pleased grin and the children all move toward the door in excitement, stumbling over each other as they had when they first came in. Annette and

Timmy yell in unison, "Gemma! Collette! Hattie! Nico's got a surprise for us!"

THE SNOW HASN'T stopped by the time the children get dressed for the cold, a sign his father's deliveries are going as smoothly as they have every other year. Nico leads the children out past the covered pool and starts them on their walk through the grounds. It's a more direct route than taking them to the private road leading to the back of their property, and though it's been snowing all morning, it's not accumulated enough to make it difficult for the children to walk through. It'll be quicker this way.

Their eyes are wide with wonder as they trek through the snow, stopping every so often to throw snowballs at each other, and the sight of it allows Nico to block out the nervous energy he's accumulated since arriving back here. As they narrow in on the barn, the kids beam at him with realization, and Nico's mind is finally free, at least for a moment, from the worry plaguing him.

Collette and Hattie, who are dressed from tip to toe in layers of the warmest clothes they own, are bouncing on the balls of their feet, red-nosed and sniffling. They're the adopted daughters of his eldest sister, Joy, and her wife, Eloise, and have absolutely none of the magical protections against the cold the rest of their cousins inherited as the biological grandchildren of Santa Claus. Nico planned to make a show of their entrance, but the temperature appears to be getting the best of the rest of the children, too, even with their enhanced resilience toward the cold. He takes pity on them all, not having any idea what it's like to not be perfectly warm at all times, and slides the door to the barn open. "Are you ready to see Santa's Workshop?"

They step through the barn door into a world full of whimsy. Had any of them ventured out here without Nico or his father to accompany them, the barn door would have slid open to show a dusty old interior with a rundown tractor in the back corner. But instead, with Nico at their side, they're met at the front of Santa's Workshop by an elf wearing a crisp red suit with green trim. He looks no more than ten, but Nico knows his apparent age is deceptive; Aspen's far older than Nico will ever live to be.

"Mr. Nicholas," he squeaks. "We weren't expecting you! I would have prepared something for you and your guests."

"Aspen, it's okay," Nico soothes. "I'm only here to give the kids a little tour of the place. You know, show 'em around Santa's stomping grounds while the big guy's out for deliveries and everything's a little calmer."

Aspen's eyes widen. He glances from the giggling children, who have started to roam, to the interior of the workshop behind him, where conveyor belts haven't stopped running, and elves are still moving around with a fixed determination.

"Oh," Nico grimaces, realizing his mistake. This used to be his favorite spot. He'd spend hours wandering around, pestering the elves on their work and dreaming of the day he'd get to be in charge. But things change. "I'm sorry. It's been years since I've been out here. I forgot—" He motions around the room, from the group of elves monitoring the movement of a flashing red sleigh across a large digital map of the world to the clean-up crews near each conveyor belt, and sighs in shame. "—the workshop is still busy on delivery day. We can go. I can bring them back after Christmas."

Aspen looks horrified now. "No! I can't let you do that."

Before Nico has time to insist, Aspen is rummaging through his pocket and holding a hand up to silence him. "I can't very well turn the heir apparent away from his own workshop!"

Aspen's voice is so high Nico doesn't even bother telling him it's not yet his. At this point, it's futile. He stands there and watches as Aspen speaks into the walkie-talkie he pulled from his pocket, calling for a volunteer to show the children around.

"I know you could show them around yourself." Aspen answers before the question is even out of Nico's mouth. "But groups of three or more are supposed to be led by a senior elf when Santa's not in the workshop, and well…"

"I'm not yet Santa," Nico finishes.

"Exactly! So since there's so many of you"—Aspen says, gaze once again darting around all the kids Nico brought with him—"you're going to need an official tour guide."

Nico purses his lips to keep from groaning. That can't be a real rule. He swears it was made up to keep him and his sisters from annoying the elves while he wasn't around. But then, he could never sense it was a lie when his father said it to them when they were younger—and unlike his sisters, he'd be able to tell if it were—so the rule must be legitimate.

Nico can't hold his groan in any longer, murmuring under his breath "What a ridiculous rule."

Aspen doesn't hear him, too busy trying, and mostly failing, to get the children to come back to the front of the workshop as they wait for their guide.

He gives up, shoulders slumping as he squeaks, "I have no idea how Mr. Kristoff does it. Children are exhausting!"

Nico suppresses a laugh. He takes pity and calls the kids back, and they come immediately.

Aspen shakes his head, dejected.

"It's a Santa thing, Aspen. Kids flock to them."

Aspen jumps, voice cracking, "My Dickens, Chrysanthemum! You startled me."

She pats his shoulder. "Everything startles you, dear."

That doesn't surprise Nico; a mouse could spook Aspen. Chrysanthemum, on the other hand, is the opposite of Aspen in almost every way. They share the same lilac eyes and eternal youth all elves do, but where Aspen is awkward and timid, Chrysanthemum holds herself with all the grace and poise to be expected from an immortal being born from snow. And though she's no taller than the twins, the oldest of Nico's nieces and nephews, none of the children bat an eye when she claps her hands together and says, "All right, little ones, are you ready to see where all the Christmas magic begins?"

There are cheers all around. Gemma, Carol's oldest, is nearly knocked over by the force with which Max tries to get down from her arms. He runs over to Chrysanthemum and grabs her hand. He's so excited, bouncing at her side on the balls of his feet, that everything he's trying to say only comes out as an indecipherable babble. Chrysanthemum has no problem understanding him, though, nodding her head as she answers, "Yes, this *is* where all the toys are made."

She leads him away from the foyer, where Nico and the children gathered with Aspen while waiting, and the rest of the children follow like little ducks in a row. Aspen stares after them in awe and then turns to Nico and says, "She's almost as good with kids as you and your father are, sir."

Nico is taken aback by the formality, covering his laugh with a cough. "Please call me Nico, Aspen. No need to call me 'sir.'"

"Right, si-Nico. Is there anything else I can help you with?" He examines his watch and frowns. "I must get back to taking inventory."

"No, I'll be..." He trails off, motioning around the room as a tremor of sadness builds up inside him again.

"Right," Aspen says, clapping his hands together and smiling. Nico's shift in mood is entirely lost on him. "I'm off to see what this year's Christmas did for our supplies. We mustn't delay restocking if we want to keep the cogs running."

Nico nods, calling after him, "Sorry again for interrupting!"

In response, Aspen waves his hand in the air and scurries off. He doesn't seem too bothered by the interruption, and Nico smiles, but it's fleeting. He thought coming to the workshop would liven his mood, but instead, it's only made him gloomier. There's so much about this place, and the things he once loved it for, he's forgotten. He checks the children are still enthralled by Chrysanthemum's tour and then steps outside, back into the world he's always called home. He slides the door shut, sinks into the snow at the foot of it, and slouches against the barn. His head hits the weathered wood, too hard. He winces.

Avoidance seemed to be the best decision at the time. Now, with a year left until he has to deal with the realities of the situation, Nico realizes he should have dealt with it head-on. At the very least, he should have found out what happens to the family business when an heir deviates from the norm. He has a year to fall in love and be loved in return and such a feat is already daunting enough without the added pressure of revealing his family secret. The idea of telling someone he cares for, someone he loves enough to ignite the Santafication process, Santa Claus is not only real, but *he's* the next in line to take over makes his stomach churn. It spikes his anxiety even higher than the idea of telling his father he's gay. At least with coming out, his father knows queer people exist. Despite everyone on earth possessing their own magic, people don't believe in Santa

Claus past a certain age. As they grow older, they no longer speak of Santa, and Nico fears he won't be able to broach the subject outside his family without sounding ridiculous.

Nico pinches the bridge of his nose. It was a mistake to come here. It wasn't a distraction at all. In fact, seeing the inside of the workshop after so long serves as a reminder of all the joy and happiness he's denied himself over the years out of fear of rejection. Rejection from his father for not being straight and jeopardizing the Santa line. Rejection from his family as a whole for keeping this truth from them. Rejection from a hypothetical partner for daring to say something as ridiculous as the truth of who he is and what he's expected to become. He can't stop the tears. He's been overwhelmed by the idea of rejection for as long as he can remember, but the reality of how soon it may come terrifies him. It's a crushing weight on his chest, nearly tangible in its magnitude.

There's so much to do. So much to risk. So much he has to put out into the world before he can even become Santa Claus, and Nico's not ready for any of it. At all. He's avoided commitment for so long, never allowing himself to get close enough to fall in love, and now it's apparent he may have done nothing but set himself up for failure. He's already defeated, and he didn't even begin. He wipes the tears from his eyes and stands, wishing for once he could get cold so he'd have the weather to blame for his new-found redness. He shakes his hair out, runs a hand over his face, and slides the barn door open again, mumbling as he steps back inside, "Get it together, Nicholas. You've got a job to do."

He joins Chrysanthemum and the children at the back of the workshop where they're standing in front of a large, intricate set of crystal doors. Nico smiles, remembering the rush of awe he experienced the first time his father pushed these doors open and showed him the North Pole outside the confines of the workshop magically contained in their barn. He imagines his face mimicked the faces of his nieces and nephews right now. Eyes wide and mouths falling open as Chrysanthemum pushes the grand doors open and ushers the children through them. "And here is the Northern Realm in its entirety. Or, as it's known to humans, the North Pole. It's a world of dreams and wishes and magic, and it's the most beautiful place you'll ever see."

Nico's father, Kristoff, said nearly the same thing to him when he first crossed the threshold into the Northern Realm. At the time, he believed it without hesitation; he was seven and couldn't imagine a single thing more beautiful than an otherworldly realm of unmitigated magic. Now, more than twenty years later, with years of traveling under his belt, he knows it to be true. There is nothing on this earth that compares to the Northern Realm.

Chrysanthemum motions for the children to follow and steps farther into the powdery white landscape. As she walks, the indentations she's left behind disappear, and the snow is once again soft and pristine, as if it's freshly fallen. Gemma points to the ground as the children follow behind Chrysanthemum, squealing as all their footprints vanish before her eyes. "How is this happening?"

"Magic," Nico explains. "Isn't it wonderful? The snow never gets gross here. It's always perfect and new."

Timmy and Annette run forward and flop into a sea of white. As they brush themselves off, they watch in awe as the impressions their bodies made smooth out before either of them can finish saying, "This is amazing!"

The allure of this realm is lost on them; they're all too busy playing in the self-replenishing flakes to even acknowledge the world beyond it. Nico can't blame them as he was much the same on his first visit, but every visit after, he grew more enamored with the charming village and its mesmerizing beauty. But even then, when he couldn't imagine wanting anything other than being Santa Claus, it was too small, a little too stifling to be called home. The quaintness of the Northern Realm was a constant reminder of what his life was meant to be, of what parts of his world he'd have to give up in order to step into his father's. It was a daunting thing to grapple with as he grew up—the fact a place so beautiful, so wonderful, so full of magic, could cause him so much anxiety.

It's bigger now—the cabins on the main street stretching farther back toward the mountains than they had the last time he visited, but even so, Nico's stomach clenches and then flutters in an all too familiar way. He's overwhelmed. The village might have grown in his absence, but it fills him with the same suffocating dread as the last time he visited. He'd been twenty-two and angry, resentment and frustration bubbling inside him enough to dim the beauty of the Northern Realm. Today isn't much different; he takes in the perfectly picturesque town in front of him and all he sees is the confinement and restraint he did then. The view brings him no joy, leaving him with the same ache of anxiety, instead. He falls back as the children follow Chrysanthemum and he presses the heels of his hands against his eyes, trying to stave off the memory. It doesn't work. His stomach turns sour and bile rises in his throat as he remembers.

Kristoff had spent the morning telling Nico all the things expected of him now that he'd graduated. He made a point to emphasize how it was fine while he was in college to not think seriously of love, but as one chapter of his life closed another must open. How it was imperative for the next part to be one of buckling down and seriously thinking about commitment. Nico had already been on edge that day: the guy he'd been seeing wanted more and Nico had balked. He couldn't commit to anything serious—not then, not now, maybe not ever—so he'd broken it off. It stung for his father to remind him, without even realizing what he was doing, why he ended it. His father and all his expectations were a constant reminder as to why Nico pushed every man he ever started to fall for away. It was too much then, definitely too much now, and Nico snapped.

He told Kristoff he wanted nothing to do with being Father Fucking Christmas and stormed out of the house like a petulant child. It wasn't his best look, but Kristoff didn't come after him and that only made him angrier. He went to the workshop to cool off, walked through the Northern Realm, and cried in frustration because this is all he wanted when he was younger, and now it was a burden. Shortly after, he moved out and started avoiding the house at all costs, only making a point to come back for Christmas. He would have skipped those visits, too, if it hadn't been for his growing family and the joy it brought to his sisters and their children when he showed up. If he had to grit his teeth and bear it as his father gave him yet another lecture on embracing his destiny before it was too late, then he would, for them. The big, bright smiles on the kids' faces when they opened their gifts made it all worthwhile in the end.

But now, walking through the Realm and watching the kids play in the snow, Nico understands all he did was deny himself that same joy. Avoiding his responsibilities hasn't stopped the cogs of this long-running machine, it only put more pressure on him to fulfill his destiny in a shorter, more pressing, amount of time. He realizes now all he's jeopardized by skirting his responsibilities this long. What if he can't find love? What if he honestly can't become Santa Claus? What if he ruins Christmas for every child in the world by ending the Santa line? Now that it seems to be a reality, Nico is panicking. He doesn't actually want to not be Santa Claus, does he?

"Nico!" Gemma yells right before he's hit with a snowball. It draws him out of his thoughts and he laughs when he sees Annette pointing at Timmy before he can even ask who threw it.

Timmy laughs, too, calling out, "You're not even paying attention!"

That's true. He'd been too distracted by memories of the past and fears for the future to keep up with their adventure.

He wipes the snow from his sweater. "Sorry, Timmy. What have I missed? Has Chrysanthemum been telling you anything interesting? Did she tell you she's older than all of us put together?"

"What?"

"How is that possible?"

"You're lying!"

"She's looks our age!"

Chrysanthemum hides a laugh behind her hand as the children talk over each other, all in a state of shock at what Nico told them.

"It's magic," she says. "But follow me and I'll show you where it all began."

She leads them farther down to the roundabout at the center of Main Street, where the village starts to expand off to the right and left. Above the center of the roundabout floats a giant, rotating snowflake. It appears to be a perfectly smooth ice sculpture, but Nico knows no person had anything to do with its creation.

Chrysanthemum points up to it, explaining, "This is the source of all the Northern Realm's powers. It's where your grandfather and your dear uncle Nico get theirs, or at least the ones not of earth. It's where we elves get our magic and, of course, where we're born."

"You're born *here*?" Collette gives voice to the disbelief written across the children's faces.

"It's too cold," Hattie says at the same time Gemma says, "But there's no hospital here."

Chrysanthemum smiles, amused by their confusion, and Nico rolls his eyes, muttering, "You could have led with something simpler."

Chrysanthemum purses her lips. "Children can understand anything if you explain it well enough."

Nico breathes out through his nose, sharp and frustrated, but doesn't say anything as Chrysanthemum continues, unfazed. "This is the heart of the Northern Realm: the very first snowflake from which all other snow proceeds and all our magic originates."

She points to the core of the snowflake, where it's shimmering with a gently pulsing blue light. "See there? That's where I came from many, many moons ago. As your world's population gets bigger and Santa needs more help making presents, the Great Flake rises up into the sky and makes millions of little snowflakes fall to the ground. Upon landing, some of them turn into elves like me, fully grown and ready to spread the magic of Christmas. The rest stay as they are and keep the Northern Realm full of magic."

"Wow," Timmy says as Annette and the twins ooh and ah.

"Is that why our footprints never stay put?" Gemma asks, "Because it's full of magic?"

"Yes, absolutely. The snow here can do so many wonderful things because it's a magical kind, not a weather kind."

The kids nod in agreement and Max claps his hands in excitement, nearly shouting, "Magical!"

"And it never gets cold," she adds, her eyes twinkling with mirth. "But you all were so excited to play in the snow I don't think you noticed the earthly misconception about the Northern Realm being frigid isn't even true."

Hattie and Collette, who are the least adept at dealing with the cold, turn to each other in shock, pointing at each other as they say in unison, "We never put our layers back on!"

"I love this place!" Annette says and Timmy turns to Nico, almost whining, "Why don't we live here?"

Chrysanthemum crosses her arms and lets Nico answer, face turned up in expectation as if she doesn't already know. "Well, originally we did."

Timmy's face falls and Nico remembers the mixture of disappointment and relief he felt learning that fact too. He points down the street to the large house on the hill. "That's where the very first Santa Claus lived when he accepted his post from the elves. But then the world grew and technology advanced, and Santas, because we're only human, grew tired of the isolation."

Nico sighs, the next part made sense to him as a child, but now that he's living it, he hates it in a way he never thought he would. "And it ultimately became much more difficult for the Santa line to continue, for our ancestors to meet and fall in love with their partners—"

Chrysanthemum quirks an eyebrow at his word choice, and Nico blushes, stumbling over his words as he continues. "When it—when they only had limited time on earth outside of Delivery Day."

"Hmm," Timmy hums, considering Nico's explanation. "I guess that makes sense. Mommy probably would have never met Daddy if she lived here forever. But it would have been *sooo* cool if she did."

He then turns to his cousins and asks, "Can you imagine living here? Would we even have to go to school?"

Timmy's question sets the six of them off in excited contemplation. As they huddle together to discuss the benefits of living here in the Northern Realm permanently versus where they live now with their parents, Nico makes a point not to make eye contact with Chrysanthemum. He's always thought she knew he wasn't interested in girls, but now he's sure of it. The moment she raised her eyebrow when he chose the word partners instead of wives he felt the rush of knowing wash over him, the same familiar gut feeling that starts in his stomach and radiates outward and can only be explained as the physical manifestation of Santa's intuition.

Elves, like all Santas, are keenly perceptive beings, and if Chrysanthemum knows, Nico wonders how successful his mission to keep his sexuality from his father has been all these years. It's something he's always had to grapple with, something always subconsciously worrying him. Now that he's planning to tell his parents, though, he doesn't know if he wants his father to have picked up on something he let slip when he was around more often, using his magic to confirm he's always been lying about being interested in women, or if he wants it to be a surprise, wants him to not have realized at all. His heart rate kicks up at the idea of his father knowing this entire time and still stressing the need for him to find a wife. If he's honest with himself, he'd much prefer his father to have been oblivious. Nico wouldn't be able to handle knowing his father knew and deliberately made the last decade of his life miserable. There'd be no mending fences after learning such a thing.

Chrysanthemum touches his hand, drawing him out of his thoughts. Her voice is hushed but firm, eyes steely with conviction. "Nicholas Hamurişi, you are full of magic, and magical things will happen to you if only you open your heart to the possibilities."

He wants to snap back, tell her it's easy for her to say. He wants to tell her it must be nice to unwaveringly believe in the power of magic. He wants to say so many things, but the words get caught in his throat as she continues. "Everything will work out wonderfully for you. I know things. I'm an elf, after all."

Her smile is warm and comforting, and Nico is reassured some positivity will follow from telling his family who he is and who he loves. Because, ultimately, all he wants is for his family to accept him. Making his love life work with his duties as the heir to the sleigh would only be an added bonus.

Chapter Three

AFTER NICO AND the children return from the barn, he and his sisters spend the rest of the day helping their mother prepare for tomorrow morning's postdelivery brunch while the spouses keep the kids entertained with making crafts and cards for Kristoff's return. Nico ends the day by taking a long, hot shower, as if the heat from the water will wash away the anxiety building up inside him. He locks himself in his room without saying good night to anyone and hopes sleep will bring peace from the jumbled thoughts whirring around his brain. He's barely slept since he got in, only the small nap after he arrived, but despite the bone-deep exhaustion seeping through him, his mind won't quiet. He tosses and turns for a long while before he manages to slip into sleep, and even then, it's restless and full of nightmares.

In the morning, he's once again woken by a knock on the door. This time it actually is Timmy.

"Uncle Nico! Uncle Nico," he shouts through the door.

Nico pulls himself out of bed, body aching after a terrible night, and opens the door, schooling his face in a smile for Timmy. "Good morning. What a nice wake-up call you are. What time is it? "

"It's nearly eleven!"

Nico tries not to wince at the pitch of Timmy's voice, but a stress headache is forming.

"Did your mother send you to wake me? I guess eleven is a bit late to be sleeping on Christmas morning,"

"Exactly! But it wasn't Mommy who sent me to wake you," Timmy says, and this time Nico does wince when he finishes his sentence. "It was Grandpa."

Nico runs his hands through his hair and takes a deep breath. Oversleeping and frustrating his father is definitely how he wanted to start his morning. It's the perfect foot to put forward the day he's supposed to come out.

"Well, we don't want to keep the big guy waiting, do we?"

Timmy smiles, not picking up on the tone in Nico's voice or his wary expression. He turns, running toward the stairs, and Nico calls after him, "Tell everyone I'm getting dressed and then I'll be down!"

Nico's the last one to arrive downstairs. Everyone's already gathered around the formal dining room table, where the food is laid out on his mother's very best china. All eyes, except for his father's, turn toward him as he enters the room and he grimaces, hoping they hadn't been waiting too long. The pointed way in which his father won't even glance his way tells him any amount of time waiting was too much.

"Merry Christmas," he greets. "Sorry I overslept."

Noelle, always the thoughtful one, appears to have saved him a seat next to hers. Unfortunately, it's also right next to his father's.

Murmurs of platitudes from his siblings and excited calls from his nieces and nephews greet him as he passes them on his way toward his father, whose disappointment hit him the moment he stepped in the room. His parents' giant dining room table has never felt so long until this moment.

Kristoff raises his head. The spot on the table he's been staring at since Nico entered the room no longer holds his attention and Nico's hand falters on his seat. He may be twenty-nine, but his father's gaze affects him as much now as it did when he was little. Kristoff's eyes are tired, huge purple-gray bags blooming beneath them from the strain of his immense delivery route.

"We missed you Saturday, Nicholas." Kristoff's voice is weary and tight, a key indication it's not only the twenty-six hours of global deliveries, with a mere nap to recoup, causing his exhaustion. Nico averts his eyes, studying the place setting before him as he mumbles, "It won't happen again."

They share a look, and Nico is uncomfortably aware of Kristoff trying to pick up on whether he's lying or not. But it's only a lie if Nico knows it to be untrue, which he doesn't—his statement depends on how the year goes. He can't be sure at this point that he won't skip another predelivery dinner, but he doesn't need to tell Kristoff all that. Though, he does hope by this time next year, he's at least managed to be on better terms with his father. Whether he's found true love or not, he'd love coming home to be more than an anxiety-inducing mess.

Kristoff nods at Nico, conceding, and then raises his champagne glass, turning his attention to the rest of the family. "Merry Christmas! Now that everyone's here, there's no need to let the food get cold."

Nico can barely contain his scoff. The food going cold around his father isn't even a possibility, especially on Christmas, but of course, facts go out the window when a point needs to be made of Nico being late. Kristoff continues without even a sideways glance at Nico's reaction. "It's been a wonderful holiday season, and I'm so pleased you could all make it out. Here's to you and another year full of blessings!"

He raises his glass higher, and the adults at the table follow, saying in unison, "Cheers!" Nico watches his nieces and nephews scattered throughout the table and smiles as they bring their plastic cups up as well. For a moment, even with his father sitting beside him and the tension radiating between the two, it's nice to be home and surrounded by family again.

Brunch is wonderful. The food is good, and the company is great, but it doesn't last nearly long enough. Before Nico's ready, the conversation dies down, and the children grow restless. Kristoff looks to Nico. His lips are smoothed into an impossibly thin line. His eyes are as tired as they had been at the start of brunch, but now they are devoid of all the mirth and joy they'd been twinkling with while the family was dining. Kristoff takes a deep breath and lets it go in a sharp exhale, none of the tension in his shoulders leaving as he does. Not that it would. This is the precursor to the Talk: the thunder before the lightning, or the warning for what's to come.

"Son," Kristoff says. His voice is tired and clipped, and Nico would know what's coming even without his heightened intuition. Nico hoped his father would wait until after Christmas to bring this up or, at the very least, wait until the rest of his family had left the room before beginning the discussion. Yet, his father is never one to make things easy for him. Nico takes a few calming breaths and braces for the emotional hailstorm to come.

"Honey," Gloria says. "We can discuss this tomorrow. Let's just celebrate the end of the season for now."

Kristoff purses his lips again, and the adults at the table, especially his sisters, tense as the children stay oblivious. One by one his sisters' spouses say their thanks for the food and whisk their chattering children off to another room for the duration of this conversation—the unspoken dismissal of everyone other than Nico and his sisters understood loud and clear.

"No," Kristoff says, leaving no room for arguing or negotiating from any of them. Joy, Belle, and Carol join them at their end of the table as their father continues. "Unfortunately, this cannot wait any longer. The final countdown has already begun, and we're running out of time."

Nico closes his eyes and tries not to lose his temper at the way his father says *we're* as if he has anything to do with this at all. He takes one more deep breath and prepares himself for another Christmas meal ending in frustration with and resentment toward his father.

"Nico, will you look at me?"

Nico opens his eyes and begrudgingly turns his attention to his father. Kristoff's face is softer now, but only subtly so. He doesn't appear to be gearing up to tell Nico off for still being single at the beginning of his thirtieth year. Instead, he seems ready to gently remind Nico of all the negative effects not finding love within the year will have on Nico and their family as a whole. At this point, Nico thinks he would prefer the former; at least then he'd be justified in the anger already boiling up inside.

"Before you ask, because I know you're dying to know, I am not seeing anyone."

It's not the best way to start the conversation—Nico knows this—but antagonizing his father is what he does best. Kristoff grits his teeth and his mother barely contains a sigh while Noelle slips her fingers through Nico's, squeezing his hand in an attempt at reassurance. Carol and Belle share a grimace, and Joy gives Nico a sympathetic smile before turning to their father and saying, "Come on Dad, he's got plenty of time to find someone to settle down with."

Nico's heart skips at her word choice, and Noelle squeezes his hand harder—she's the only one who knows, but Joy has always been the most inclusive in the way she talks about romantic interests.

"Yes," Kristoff sighs, pinching the bridge of his nose. "Of course, he has time to *find* a girl to settle down with. But does he have time to fall in love with the girl? Does he have time for the girl to love him back? Does he have time to know it's real, true, magic-inducing love before his time runs out?"

It's Nico's turn to roll his eyes but his mother chimes in before he can say an actual word.

"Kris," Gloria says, voice soothing despite the turn in conversation, "a year will be plenty of time. He'll just have to be proactive."

"Yeah," Carol chimes in. "Jay and I fell in love in an instant, or at least it seemed. I bet Nic will be exactly the same! You don't need to worry, Dad."

Wrong, Nico thinks. *He's got at least a few reasons to worry.*

Belle is nodding her head in enthusiastic agreement with Carol, which is to be expected since they always take each other's side, but she isn't given a moment to vocalize the agreement before Kristoff is raising his hand to silence them all.

"Listen, I know you all mean well, but the facts aren't in Nicholas's favor; he hasn't even stayed in one place for more than a year and a half since he turned twenty-two. I don't know how any of you expect him to settle down and fall in love if he can't even commit to a place long enough to give himself the chance to find a girl to be romantically involved with."

Nico's had enough of everyone discussing him while pretending he's not even there and he snaps. His voice is thick with the effort to stay calm.

"First of all," Nico says. "I've been in the same apartment for *years*— I just travel a lot! And second of all, can you all stop talking like my love life is some sort of reality show? As if I'm not sitting *right here!*"

No one says anything for a long moment. His mother and sisters duck their heads in shame, but his father continues to stare, not even blinking, waiting to see if his outburst will continue. Nico adds, quieter this time, in a near whine, "Also, I *have* had romantic relationships."

"But have any of them lasted?" Kristoff asks, closing his eyes for a long moment, mouth turned down in a worried frown.

"Obviously not," Nico snaps, his voice every bit as petulant as he feels, and he would be embarrassed if it weren't for how infuriating this all is.

"Nicholas," Kristoff says, curt and reprimanding. "You've never even had a serious girlfriend. How do you expect to come into your full powers and take on this job if you're not even searching for love. You know what the Santafication process entails, and you *know* what's at stake here if you don't find someone!"

Nico clenches his jaw. "Yes, I know."

Noelle gives his hand one last squeeze before pulling away and placing her hands on the table, fingers splayed out in one of her telltale signs of frustration. She's had enough of the conversation as well, but unlike Nico, she doesn't have a stake in this race. She can speak her mind more freely, without fear of giving up too personal information in the wrong moment. Nico rubs the palms of his hands against the fabric of his jeans, willing himself to calm down and face the conversation head-on. He misses the warmth of Noelle's hand in his—its absence makes him feel smaller than he had the moment before—because at least then he'd had a physical reminder that despite the discussion at hand his sister would always be there for him.

Some days he feels silly for all the ways he's grown to rely on Noelle to get him through these sorts of situations but not today. Not now as his father stares him down, years of disappointment and concern over Nico's commitment to the family business written all over his face. Noelle is small in stature but makes up for it in personality. She's loud and boisterous and as strong-willed as Kristoff. Her personality is the only one in the family big enough to counter their father's and maybe it's because of that quality, or because she's so deeply protective of all of them, that she's the only one who will consistently go toe to toe with Kristoff during a family meeting.

She takes a deep breath, smiles softly, and tucks a black curl behind her ear. Nico doesn't know exactly what she's thinking, but her eyes are sparkling, and he's hit square in the chest by the wave of determination radiating from her. She must have concocted some sort of plan of her own, which should be interesting considering her track record as far as viable plans go. Though no matter what the plan is, Nico is thankful when she starts speaking if only for the reprieve it gives him from his father's attention.

"Dad, Dad, Daddy," she says, familiarly playful. There's a hint of goading to her tone, though, enough to indicate to everyone she's prepared for an argument if need be. "You needn't worry about Nic's love life. We've already got a plan to get the ball rolling."

Kristoff raises an eyebrow at Noelle, and then his eyes dart to Nico before he can fully suppress the confused expression washing over his face.

This isn't good, Nico thinks. *He literally knows when people lie!*

"Really?" Kristoff asks, his voice conveying every bit of apprehension Nico is feeling.

Noelle is not deterred and assures Kristoff she does indeed have a plan. The following silence does nothing to calm Nico's nerves. His parents and remaining sisters turn to each other in search of an answer to what's not being said, as if any of them know what Noelle is up to. Noelle never looks away from Kristoff and neither does Nico. He and his father are the only two at the table with heightened intuition, and while he knows Noelle is scheming, his father doesn't seem to think she's lying. This is a good sign, but still. Trying to fool their father is a very delicate task, and while Noelle has always been the best at it, Nico isn't confident she'll succeed, not when his father's already so on edge.

After glancing around the table one last time, Kristoff's gaze settles back on Noelle, and finally, with every bit of his tone conveying he's as prepared for an argument as Noelle, he says, "Do tell, then."

Nico breathes in deeply, forcing his face into a picture of calm, and silently pleads: *Dear god, let this be a good plan.*

"Well, first I should probably be up-front..."

His father's mouth twitches, a near imperceptible movement, and Nico's stomach plummets. This can't be good. He's so worried he almost doesn't catch the rest of Noelle's words.

"It's actually my and Noah's plan. Nico hasn't actually agreed to it yet, but I think he will in the end."

His father's eyes widen, his surprise clear as day, and Nico knows Noelle's won. She's made it to where Nico not knowing the plan isn't a lie; his father won't be able to know by magic Nico's finding this out at the same time as he is.

She has always been the best at this, and he never should have doubted her.

"Noah and I have been talking, and we think it'll be a good idea for Nico to move into our garage apartment in Pine Cove for the duration of the countdown."

Maybe he was right to doubt her after all.

There's a ripple of confusion around the table and Gloria speaks first. "Pine Cove? Honey, I know you love your home, but Nico's been living in big cities since he left home. Do you honestly believe such a place is the best fit for him right now?"

His mother has a point. Nico can't think of settling down in a town as small as Pine Cove, even if it's only for a year, but especially not when he's supposed to be finding true love on a deadline. Noelle is speaking again, but he's only partially paying attention, too caught up in contemplating whether or not he could actually make this move.

"I know it's not what he's used to, but he can work at Kahveci's with us so he doesn't seem like a trust-fund kid living off Daddy's money—"

His brain catches up.

"Hey," Nico pouts, and his sisters laugh. There's a twinkle in Kristoff's eyes, and Gloria ducks her face behind her hand, covering a smile. "I have a job!"

"Of course, you do," Belle says, teasing. "But freelance photography isn't exactly a steady source of income, is it? It's not like the family inheritance hasn't helped you maintain your lifestyle."

Noelle waves her hand, brushing off Belle's comments and stopping Nico, or anyone else, from chiming in further. She clears her throat and glances around the table expectantly, demanding their attention return to her without so much as saying a word. "Anyway, he'll have a job and—" Her mouth twists into a smug smile, eyes bright, and Nico's stomach swoops as she finishes her sentence. "—it just so happens the tenant who lives above our shop would be perfect for him."

That makes everyone perk up, especially his father. Nico can't imagine how Noelle would know his type, let alone who would be perfect for him when she just found out he's gay. But she very clearly said tenant instead of *woman,* and he can't pick up on any lies, and for an instant, Nico allows himself to hope this tenant—this guy, Noelle wouldn't lead him on this way—is someone he could love.

Belle and Carol squeal, always so easily excitable, and Joy says, "Tell us about them."

Nico closes his eyes for a moment, a soft smile playing at his lips against his will. Joy, and her penchant for using gender-neutral language in cases of the unknown, has given Noelle the perfect avenue to continue this conversation without giving away Noah's secret. He has to clamp his mouth shut, bite the inside of his cheek to keep from sighing in relief. He'll have to thank Joy one day.

Noelle turns to him, raising an eyebrow, asking him how she should proceed without saying anything at all. He wants to nod, subtle and barely perceptible so only she can see. He wants to give her permission to keep this conversation going, to watch her tiptoe around his secret while appeasing their father with her plan. But he thinks this might be the perfect opportunity. Now is as good a time as any, maybe even better than most, to tell everyone what's made him so reluctant to fulfill his destiny.

Nico takes a long, deep breath and lets it out as slowly as he can. It does nothing to soothe the buzz of anxiety coursing through his body or the erratic beating of his heart in his ears. It's now or never, so he talks, words coming out in a jumble. "Okay. Um. I have an announcement. Before we, uh, continue this topic further. I think it'll maybe, um, clear some things up for everyone."

He's nervous. His palms are sweaty and his throat tightens as the attention of his family turns to him. He should have let Noelle keep talking. At least, then, he'd only have to be vaguely aware of what was going on instead of fully and totally in control.

He clears his throat, takes a sip of his forgotten mimosa, now too warm, and grimaces. "Okay. Well. I might as well get right to the point. I'm not interested in finding the right *girl*. There is no Mrs. Right, nor will there ever be one or whatever, because I'm gay."

Gloria's eyes widen. Carol and Belle glance at each other and then at Nico. Kristoff's mustache twitches, but his expression is otherwise imperceptible. Noelle gives his arm a quick, reassuring pat, and Joy, wearing a huge, warm smile, is the first to speak.

"Oh, Nico." She touches her hand to her mouth. Nico senses the happiness radiating from her even before she reaches across the table and squeezes his hand. "I'm so glad you've decided to tell us. I'm so proud of you."

Joy came out to the family more than two decades ago. Nico had been seven, and she'd just come home from her first semester at college, and he hadn't thought anything of it. He could tell she was nervous, but he didn't understand why. He didn't feel any which way about girls then either, but he could see why his friends, and Joy, would like them; lots of them were pretty. Now that it's his turn, and he is going through the same thing she had, he understands the nerves. He even had the benefit of knowing his family was accepting, Joy had paved the way for him, and still he was buzzing out of his skin saying the words. He can only imagine how much more intense it must have been to take the plunge without knowing what their parents would think.

Kristoff clears his throat and speaks slowly, carefully. "Nicholas, I apologize for…" He trails off, gaze darting to Gloria and then back to Nico, and Nico can tell how much he means it. He scrubs a hand over the scruff of his beard and continues, "For centering this whole matter…your love life and love interests on women and making it to where you felt obligated to keep this part of yourself a secret from us."

It's a huge relief for Nico to hear the regret in his father's voice, to hear him actually apologize for making things so difficult for him over the years. Nico ducks his head, revels in the warm, acceptance for a moment, and then turns his thoughts back to the task at hand. This is his father, after all, so there's no way this is the end of the discussion. There's still so much to be said here, and despite his father's best efforts, Nico knows he can't stop thinking of the deadline. He knows the future of their family line is always on his father's mind, and at the end of the day, this changes nothing. And if it does, it only makes it more pressing for Nico to get a move on.

"I didn't know how you'd react, considering…"

He can't bring himself to finish the thought, but he knows the unspoken concern regarding the need for an heir is understood, at least by his father.

Kristoff nods, rubbing his hands over his face. His shoulders slump, and his brow furrows with the weight of concentration, and Nico's nerves start to flare up again. He knows there's no way he'd have to marry a woman. The whole thing, him coming into his powers and the completion of the Santafication, relies on true love and mutual commitment—there's no faking or working your way around it. But the heir? Having a son is where things get tricky. Needing to continue the family line is what's concerned Nico for the longest time because...

"Adoption's out, isn't it?"

It's Joy who asks, and of course it is, Hattie and Collette were adopted by her and Eloise when they were two.

"It must be," Belle says. "How would the inheritance of the powers happen? Would it even be possible to pass them on without the child being biological?"

"I don't know," Kristoff admits. "But I would assume your concerns are right. The child would probably need to be biological to inherit our gifts and then take over responsibilities himself one day."

Nico rests his face in his hands and tries not to scream. He knows this comes with the territory of being the heir apparent, but he wishes, this once, everything didn't have to come back to an heir and succession and family duty. He just came out to the most important people in his life, and all they can talk about is a child he's never considered, in more than an abstract kind of way.

"For fuck's sake," Noelle says and Gloria gasps. "Sorry, Mom, but come on. Our family has been in the Santa business since forever. There is *no way* Nico is the first one to be interested in men. There's no way. There's *got* to be precedent for what happens here."

"Aren't there books? Stuff gets passed down after the Ceremony, right?" Carol asks. "Shouldn't they have some information on all this?"

"Or couldn't you ask the elves? Chrysanthemum would know, wouldn't she?" Belle adds, and Nico's stomach flutters with appreciation at the way his sisters are coming to his defense.

Nico looks up, trying to gauge his father's response. He seems less stressed than Nico expected. His voice betrays none of the emotions Nico can feel radiating off him. "Yes, there's some personal journals from previous generations and a few books detailing the infusion of magic from the Northern Realm into the first of our line that the elves have bestowed upon us."

Kristoff rubs a hand over his mouth, and his eyes fall shut for a moment. He appears so weary Nico almost regrets laying all this on him right after a delivery. When he straightens up, there's a determined set to his jaw, and he says, "I will consult with Chrysanthemum. You're right. She would be the one to know if there was precedence, but I am not particularly hopeful on that front. I know the family tree by heart, and there's never been a Santa who didn't marry a woman."

Nico's heart lurches, and Kristoff gives him a sympathetic sort of smile before he turns to Gloria and sighs, nearly laughing, "Dear, it seems our busy season might not be over yet. We've got some reading to do."

"Of course, anything for Nico," she says, and the warmth of acceptance courses through Nico again. This is good. It's gone far better than he ever thought it would.

"And obviously, this is very far in the future and only a preliminary answer," his mother says after a small moment of silence passes over them as they process the information Nico's unloaded on them. "But I think surrogacy would be the most logical conclusion to this question."

Nico perks up, hopeful for the first time in a long while. He'd never even considered surrogacy. The bubble of hope only grows as his father nods in agreement.

"We'll have to do some reading and consult the elves, but yes, I think it's a realistic option." Kristoff claps his hands together, indicating a shift in conversation is to come. "Okay, now that that's mostly settled…" He turns to Noelle, "Describe this tenant above your coffee shop. What's he like?"

"Dad," Nico draws out, and his sisters laugh at the way he slips into whining while Gloria pushes lightly at Kristoff's arm, admonishing, "Honey."

"Son," Kristoff says, mimicking Nico's tone. "This is important. We spent all this time talking about your future son, which who knows if you'll even have one on the first go. Will you be up for multiple surrogacies if that's the case? Will your partner? There's so much to discuss! But for now, it's on the backburner. You have less than a year to find a partner who is coming into something huge. You don't even have any prospects!"

"I know, Dad. I know. Which is why I'm apparently moving to Pine Cove. There's a man there *perfect for me.*"

He's laughing to keep from screaming; he went stir-crazy the last time he visited Noah and Noelle for more than a week. He can't imagine not going out of his mind with boredom, living in such a small town for an entire year. But Noelle's eyes are sparkling with joy, and his father seems astonished by his decision, and Nico thinks maybe, just maybe, he can do it. He at least has to give it a shot, considering Kristoff is right—he has absolutely no prospects at this point in time.

Chapter Four

THE REST OF Christmas Day passes in a haze. Gloria forces Kristoff to go to bed and rest before he starts in on any research; he's begrudging, but he goes as Gloria grabs his hand and pulls him away from the table. He and his sisters follow shortly after his parents, and Nico gives them all permission to tell their spouses what they've learned, and then he climbs the stairs, instead of following his sisters to join their families, and shuts himself in his room to think things through. There's too much to process, so much has transpired. His mind is whirring with anticipation and frustration and the tiniest bit of hope. Noelle didn't give him much to go off on this guy, but she says he's kind and cute and a little clumsy. She makes a point to mention he's been at nearly every Valentine's Day event her and Noah have hosted at Kahveci's, and he flirts with *everyone* there, not just the women. Nico has to admit he does seem promising.

It all seemed so absurd when Noelle first suggested it. Nico had never considered moving to a place with less than five thousand people before now, but then his father mentioned his concerns over the dating pool not being large enough in a town the size of Pine Cove, and Nico warmed to the idea. He can't help it if disagreeing with his father is always a primary motivator in his life. He's had no luck, not that he's ever actually tried, connecting with anyone at home or the places he travels, so he doesn't see how narrowing the playing field would hurt.

Well, he can. But he's not going to tell his father he agrees with him.

Besides, if he has to find love before the Christmas of his thirtieth year, he might as well do it on his own terms. If it happens to get under his father's skin? Well that's only a plus—even if the decision ends up backfiring.

He falls asleep thinking of his father telling him "I told you so" and wakes up from his nap drenched in sweat. He dreamed the entire Northern Realm melted after the Great Flake burst into flames when he failed to find love by next Christmas. It takes him a long while to recover from the nightmare, for his heartbeat to steady and for his skin to cool down. When he does manage to shake the dread long enough to leave his room, the first person he sees is Eloise.

Her smile is as warm and kind as Joy's, and the hug she greets him with is firm and comforting. "Nico, I'm so glad to hear the news. Joy and I are obviously so proud of you, but we're also so happy for you to be able to live your truth to the fullest with us and the rest of your family at your side."

Her words are a warm, comforting blanket, making him feel good and safe. It was an interesting experience being out to so many people he knows, even acquaintances, but not being able to share it with his family. Now that he's felt the relief of telling those closest to him, felt the surge of support and acceptance they each radiated, it's easy for him to admit how much it was affecting him.

"It does feel nice to no longer dread slipping up about my interest in men while I'm here. Being out to everyone will definitely take a load of stress off my life. Although there's not been much to talk about. I've not—"

"Been with anyone?"

"Oh god, no. No. I have. I *have*."

Nico's mortified. His cheeks are burning, and Eloise radiates embarrassment too. He's been with men. Some he's not felt anything for beyond sexual attraction, others where feelings fizzled out after a few dates, and even a few whom he could have had a lasting connection with if he'd only opened himself to the possibility. Mostly, he's not had anything serious since college. Not since he and Taylor broke up a week after graduation when he couldn't bring himself to say I love you back. Nico wanted to—he'd thought he loved Taylor. But his hair wasn't turning silver, and his powers weren't strengthening, and he started to doubt everything he felt.

They were twenty-two and fresh out of college, and he couldn't imagine unloading his family's truth on him at the time. Thinking back, Taylor would have believed him with no problem. He always embraced the magic of their world, never once hiding his ability to manipulate the elements. Nico's sure now Taylor would have been receptive, but at the time, it felt wrong. Nico was nervous beyond belief, and he was always under the assumption when it was right, when he found the one, everything would be simple. That making this confession would be easy. But it hadn't been. So he'd lied and said he wanted a clean break from college, and he didn't think he could handle long distance once Taylor moved back home. Taylor wanted to try, but Nico insisted it wouldn't work.

His expression when Nico said they had no future haunted him for a long time after the breakup, but the hurt and heartbreak Nico could feel radiating from Taylor had stayed with him ever since. Nico still wonders what could have been if he wasn't scared out of his mind trying to open himself up to feelings without a clear sight of how they would end. Nico often wonders how life would be with

Taylor: if he would be happy, if Taylor was the one, and if his love would turn his magic on full force. But Nico never let himself open up long enough to entertain the idea then, and now, there's no use dwelling on lost love. Not when he's got a countdown to beat.

"Sorry for overstepping," Eloise mutters, drawing him out of his thoughts.

"No, you're fine." Nico laughs, dismissing her concerns with a wave of the hand. "There's been men, but no one serious for some time."

"Oooooh," she says, realizing. "There's a man who got away."

Nico snorts. "Yeah. Something like that."

Nico has a sudden urge to reconnect with Taylor. He shakes his head and pushes the thought out of his mind. There's no use going down that road—it's been far too many years.

Eloise looks sympathetic, clearly picking up on in his shift in mood, voice kind and gentle as she says, "Well, y'know, if you ever want some advice from one gay to another, Joy and I are always here. It took her forever to get her head out of her ass too."

"Of course..." he says, mind not catching up until a moment too late. "Wait!"

Eloise smirks at him, but she doesn't explain any further. She grabs his face between her hands and says, "Ugh, I'm just so happy for you!"

Then she's moving past him and up the stairs, pausing for a moment at the top to call back down, "Heads up, your Dad's in the living room with a bunch of books!"

Nico laughs, all thoughts of Taylor washed away by his father's inability to relax. Kristoff's never been one for resting on the job and what's a more important job than ensuring the family line continues on as it always has? He heads down the hall and turns toward the kitchen instead, not wanting to interrupt his father's research or get sucked into it himself. There, he finds Noelle sitting at the island countertop reading on her laptop.

She jumps when she hears Nico enter the room. "Jeez, Tico. No one's ever told you not to sneak up on a pregnant lady before?"

"You're pregnant? Since when? Who knows? Oh man, Noelle! Congratulations!"

"So excited you didn't even give me any lip for your nickname."

"Tico's better than *Santicholas*."

"Tico, Tico, Tico," she sing-songs. "It is a good one if I do say so myself."

Noelle is so pleased Nico doesn't have the heart to tell her she's the one who came up with it, so of course, she thinks it's great. Instead, he shakes his head and asks about the baby.

Noelle shrugs. "Not much to say at the moment. I'm sixteen weeks. The next appointment is the anatomy scan. Can you even tell I'm showing?"

She stands up and moves out from behind the counter so he can see her stomach. He thought nothing of it before, but she's wearing a flowy top and he can't tell at all. She frowns, "I didn't think so. How about now?"

She pulls the fabric tight against her torso, and Nico can see it now: a small bump forming on her previously flat stomach. She's always been so thin and petite that it's a charming change of pace.

"A little. It's cute."

Her frown grows into a pout. "Thanks. But I want to be showing for real already."

Nico doesn't know what the appropriate response is, so he only nods. He joins her at the island and Noelle pats him on the back. "And to your other question, everyone knows. You missed out on the big announcement from me and Noah when you skipped the predelivery dinner. And then, well, I meant to tell you after we ate, but...you know how brunch went."

She doesn't say it to guilt him for not showing up, but Nico feels it anyway. "Skipping that dinner was probably one of my worse decisions. It only made this morning more tense than it already was going to be. But hey, for a day and a half, I got to avoid talking about how I'm failing the system."

Noelle rolls her eyes, but her voice is steady and serious as she speaks. "The system is failing you, Nico."

Nico's heart swells with affection, and he tries not to let the emotion overcome him as she continues. "The world's full of magic. We've all got it in some way. You and Dad more than the rest of us, because of who you are. But you can open the door to another realm, talk to animals, tell when people are lying, and all this other cool shit, and I honestly don't think being interested in men is going to be an obstacle when you can do all that. I know it must seem so, like that sort of magic doesn't extend to you when all Dad's ever talked about is you following in his footsteps by falling in love with, and marrying, a woman and having a nice little Santa family. I understand where the fear comes from— we've not made this easy for you by assuming your interest in women—but I truly believe this is going to work out as well as it did for all the other Santas. Magic always finds a way."

"I know it does. I know."

He does but he's frustrated, and his voice betrays his emotions all too well. "But it doesn't feel like it does. You're right. Of course you're right. It'd be ludicrous if I couldn't continue the family line because I'm gay! Surrogacy has to work, right? I'd still be the father, but what if the magic isn't only passed on by my genes? What if producing a Santa heir involves the love or genes or *whatever* of both me and the person who sparked my full Santafication? And then if not, and surrogacy will work no matter what, what if Dad's right and I have to try seventy hundred times to get a boy and my husband *leaves me* because of it? There's just so much to go wrong. Of course, magic finds a way, but can it overcome all this?"

Noelle smiles, a small, sympathetic tug at the corners of her mouth. She grabs Nico's hands, lowering them back to the countertop after his wild gesticulation and gives them both a quick squeeze. "Magic always finds a way. And I'm going to keep saying it until you believe me because you need someone in your corner soothing your anxiety. Because right now you're a giant ball of nerves with a bad haircut—"

Nico inhales sharply, running his hand through his hair. It is getting a bit long, but. "Bad haircut? Rude."

Noelle brushes past his indignation, continuing as if his outburst never happened. "And this hair isn't getting you anywhere in the dating game. But besides all that, I think you're getting ahead of yourself. These are all valid concerns and something you should keep in mind, but in the meantime, while Dad's off pouring over those books to find out, I think you should probably focus on opening yourself up to love. Because you obviously haven't yet. And there's no opportunity for things to go wrong if nothing ever begins in the first place."

"Ugh," Nico grimaces. "You sound like Dad...but reasonable."

"Ha! Much to your dismay, he does make some fair points on this whole thing...*sometimes.*"

"Don't tell him that! He'll never let me hear the end of it."

"Hear the end of what?"

Nico startles, attention snapping to the source of the question. Kristoff is bounding through the kitchen with a book in hand and a perplexed expression.

"Oh, nothing."

Kristoff glances from Noelle to Nico, raising an eyebrow when his gaze falls on Nico. They both know she's lying, but Kristoff doesn't seem to think it's important enough to question further. He sets the book he came in with on the counter, pushing it toward Nico. It's open roughly halfway through, and upon closer examination of the old, yellowed pages, it appears to be a journal.

Nico picks it up and, glancing over the pages Kristoff left open, sees the entries are handwritten. It is a journal. The handwriting is messy, a little rushed, and very much in a different language. It's been a while, but Nico can still read in Turkish.

Nico looks up and Kristoff nods to the page, prompting him to read, "Go on. I found something that might help you out."

Nico's fully intrigued now. Noelle scoots in closer, shoulder to shoulder with Nico, so she can read along too.

June 21, 1856

Today we went to London for the solstice. Last year we went to Venice, which was more beautiful than London in every way. But today was nice in its own right. We went into a bakery and I saw a beautiful girl and her equally beautiful brother. They had the same heart-shaped face and chestnut brown eyes— I think they may have been twins. They were laughing at each other, both covered in a dusting of flour. The brother more so than the sister. He had flour in his hair and on his face, and I could imagine his sister being the culprit, especially the way her cheeks went red as their father peeked in from the backroom and reprimanded them for horsing around. I can't get over how beautiful they both were.

Nico doesn't read any farther. He returns his attention to his father, dazed. "There was a previous one of us who was into boys? You never mentioned it!"

Kristoff shrugs, mouth turned down in a frown. "I must admit this is the first time I'm learning of it myself. Your grandfather would be sorely disappointed, but I never did have a taste for reading the personal journals. Nikolai was— that's whose journal this was—your great-great-grandfather, but I never knew of his interest in men because all records of the family tree only show who past heirs married, and well, he married a woman, so I foolishly never thought to question otherwise."

"If he married a woman..." Nico frowns. "How does this help me?"

"Well," Kristoff starts. He pauses, takes a breath. "No one on the official tree of Santas has married anyone but a woman, so this isn't an answer to what it means for you to marry a man... Chrysanthemum is still consulting with the elves for an answer, but she pointed me toward the journals. She thought, and I agree, it might be helpful to know you're not alone in this family."

Kristoff makes a grand sweeping gesture as if he's trying to find his words in the air itself. He is so adamant in what he's saying, and Nico's heart seems to be floating right through his chest with how good it is to have his father understand him, even in the slightest.

Kristoff smiles, small, and a little reserved. "I imagine it can be isolating to deviate from how things have always been but at the very least…" He points to the journal, smiling broader now. "Nikolai's journal shows you're not the only Santa in a sea of straights."

Nico snorts, and Noelle slaps her hand on the counter as laughter bursts through her. "Dad! Oh my god! A sea of straights? Did you get that one from Eloise?"

Kristoff's mustache twitches, betraying his own snickering. "It may have been the turn of phrase she used when she was helping me and Joy go through all these things." He shrugs, unsure. "There's still a lot to go through. And I'm not certain it will lead to a definitive answer, but I thought I should try to find an answer myself while we wait to hear from Chrysanthemum. So, I'll let you know."

Nico's throat is tight, and he doesn't trust himself to speak without giving away his emotions. Instead, he nods.

Kristoff points to the journal again. "I'll leave that with you. The rest of it might be of interest to you. I don't know."

"Yeah." Nico clears his throat in an attempt to sound less froggish. "Thanks, Dad. I appreciate it."

Kristoff stalls before leaving, there's a look in his eyes telling Nico there's more he wants to say, but he doesn't bring it up. He claps his hand on Nico's shoulder and kisses Noelle on the forehead, bidding them both good night.

He listens as Kristoff's footsteps fade, signaling he's out of earshot, and then Noelle bursts out laughing, gasping through breaths. "Sea of straights! God, I'm going to have to tell Eloise he used that with you. She'll love it."

Nico snickers, but Noelle doesn't register through her own laughter he's not as committed to his own, and that's for the best. He can't explain it, but the glimmer in his father's eyes as he left the room gave him a bad feeling. His stomach is full of lead, and his hands are clammy. Whatever it is his father wanted to say—it's not going to be good.

Chapter Five

NICO DOESN'T FIND out how bad the thing his father wanted to say to him was until two mornings later. It's so early the children haven't woken and neither have most of their parents. Noah and Noelle are upstairs packing the last of their things. They were able to change their flights last minute so they could head home earlier than planned to set up the guest home for Nico while he heads back to his own apartment and squares things away for moving in with them. He insisted since they were putting him up they shouldn't have to prepare anything for him. He's perfectly capable of making the bed and stocking the fridge when he arrives, but Noelle has always been more persistent than him. Joy is in the living room, curled up on the couch with a mug in one hand and an old, tattered book in the other. There are books, journals, and even an odd scroll or two, spread out across the coffee tables; others precariously stacked on the end tables. Chrysanthemum and the elves have concluded—much like Noelle already did—the magic of the Northern Realm will not allow the Santa line to die out. They insist all Nico needs to concern himself with is finding love, and magic will sort the rest out. While it's enough to ease Nico's own anxiety, at least regarding the heir, it does nothing to quell Kristoff's and he keeps searching— desperate for more specifics. Nico would tell Joy to leave it be and let Kristoff fret on his own, but he thinks she may be searching for more instances of queer Santas as much for herself as she is for Nico, so he doesn't bother telling her to stop.

In the kitchen, his mother is seated at the table, and his father is at the stove making eggs. There's a small girl, who has one long brown braid falling down the center of her back, swinging her legs from the barstool. On the counter in front of her, there's a plate of bacon. She picks a piece up, and her voice is melodic as she says, "You did a wonderful job, Kristoff. It's perfectly crisp."

Kristoff hums his thanks, and Nico blinks the sleep out of his eyes, confused as he recognizes the voice of Chrysanthemum. He can't remember the last time he saw an elf visit them in the main house. The dread he's had since Christmas night, the one that has only dulled minutely since, returns with a vengeance the moment she turns to him. Her face is as warm and kind as always, but the tight corners of her smile sets him on edge. There's something strange going on here. He knows it.

"Good morning, Nicholas."

"Chrysanthemum, you know I've told you to call me Nico."

She smiles, and this time there's no hint of tightness. "Yes, of course. But I must say I'm awfully fond of your given name."

Everyone knows Nico hates his first name, but he doesn't say anything of the sort. There's no need to start a fight on the lack of individuality that comes with an entire line of men inheriting a derivative of one of two names. Not now, not when there's clearly something going on if Chrysanthemum has joined them for breakfast.

He grabs a piece of bacon and sits down at the table next to his mother, waiting for someone to tell him what's going on as he chews. No one does. He's going to have to ask.

"Not that I'm not pleased to see your warm elven face, Chrys, but I assume there's some Santa business to be dealt with. Since you're here and not off with the rest of the elves enjoying the postholiday season in full."

She doesn't answer. Instead, she turns to Kristoff. Nico can't see her face, but he can make out the barely perceptible nod Kristoff gives her before she jumps down from the barstool and joins him and Gloria at the table. Kristoff follows suit, placing the plates of eggs and bacon on the table and nodding toward them.

"Eat," Kristoff says.

Nico would but his father's stalling, and he wants to get this over with already.

"I'd much prefer to get the talking points out of the way before breakfast. That way, if it's bad, I can lose my appetite instead of wanting to vomit."

Chrysanthemum ducks her head. Nico thinks she might be trying not to laugh, but he can't be sure with the way her hair falls over her face and shields her features. His mother puts her mug down and looks to Kristoff, but still, he says nothing.

Nico huffs out, frustrated. His father can be so damn stubborn. He spoons some eggs onto his plate and grabs another piece of bacon. He eats. Fast. Everyone else, not so much.

Henrik comes inside before Kristoff has finished his own plate. It appears he may want to join the table for some food, but then his eyes sweep around the group. It doesn't take magical intuition to sense the tension in the room. He grabs a piece of bacon and mumbles something about washing up. Nico's not paying attention; he's staring at his father in hopes he'll finally break and tell him what the hell is going on.

Gloria sets her fork down and purses her lips. "Kristoffer. You tell him right now or I will."

Nico nearly laughs. He's only ever heard his mother call his father Kristoffer once before. He can't remember the context; he'd been so young. But he can clearly remember his father's reaction: the way his skin paled and his eyes widened. It's the same expression he's wearing right now. Kristoff is not someone Nico would call timid, but when Gloria says his name in that tone, it's the only word that fits.

Kristoff clears his throat. "Son, since I haven't found anything in the old journals, and the elves can't offer specific insight into how the magic will find a way to continue our family line, I think it's best if you have a mentor at your side on this journey."

Nico blinks. His throat is dry. It's worse than he imagined. "You want me to have a babysitter? Jesus Christ, Dad, I'm nearly thirty."

Gloria buries her head in her hands, and Chrysanthemum straightens up in the seat next to him. Nico turns to her and then to his father, astounded. "You want *Chrysanthemum* to be my babysitter?"

"Nicholas," Kristoff says. He's regained his old demeanor, any sign of timidity washed away with Nico questioning his decision. "She wouldn't be your babysitter. She is the first elf ever born from the Snow, and she has been a great asset to every single one of the Santas since the beginning. And—"

He stops abruptly and takes a deep breath. His expression is tight, and Nico's smacked in the chest with frustration. "Listen Nicholas, in the beginning, the elves were always nearby—except for when Santas were courting—and I think, since so much of this is unfamiliar, we need to go back to a similar setup. I think you will benefit greatly from having an elf by your side in this—to guide you in the way they did initially."

Nico blinks, dumbfounded. No matter the reassurance Chrysanthemum has offered him, Kristoff doubts Nico's ability to get this done on his own. He pinches the bridge of his nose, suppresses rolling his eyes, and turns to his mother for help. She shrugs, and Nico guesses she's either on Kristoff's side or, at least, trying to stay neutral in this matter. She's going to be no help at all in refuting this plan. He looks to Chrysanthemum and his anger seems far away. Elves have a way about them.

"Okay," he says. He still thinks it's a terrible idea, but he might as well go along with it. At least for now, at least until he can figure out a way to get around it. "But first, tell me how exactly I'm going to explain having someone who appears to be ten living with me? Is she supposed to be my daughter?"

There's a beat of silence. Then Kristoff purses his lips. "Oh."

"You hadn't thought of it, had you?"

"No, I hadn't. I'm so used to seeing the elves I'd forgotten people would see her as a child."

Nico didn't expect Kristoff to admit his mistake, and since he has, it takes the wind out of his sails almost entirely. He once again finds himself wanting to go along with the plan to please his father. "I can say she's my daughter from a fling from when I thought I was straight."

There was never any such fling. There was a time, a long time ago, when he hadn't realized yet the way he viewed girls was the way he was supposed to view boys—with admiration and maybe jealousy but never attraction. And though that was long before he'd been sexually active, Nico doesn't think it matters in this case.

Gloria shakes her head. "No, I don't think that's a good idea to say."

"Why not?" Nico and Kristoff ask in unison, and Gloria smiles like she's dealing with children.

"You're already going to have to reveal a lot of difficult things. Saying she's your daughter, something so simple to understand, and then yanking it away after you've revealed who you are and our family's truth will not go over well. I can't imagine anyone would want to be lied to in such a manner, even if it's Santa's son and the very first elf ever born. It will hurt them—whoever they are. I'm sure of it."

She makes a good point, and this might be exactly what Nico needs to get Kristoff to rethink shoving a babysitter on him.

"What if you say I am your adopted sister," Chrysanthemum suggests. "You can say your parents are taking a well-needed vacation from the toy business, and they thought it would best to keep me in school while they traveled, so you volunteered to take me in for the duration."

That does seem more reasonable than Nico having a ten-year-old daughter. But. "The move? Why wouldn't I go to you instead of us going to Noelle?"

Kristoff's eyes light up. "You've gone to help Noelle set up for the baby! She's pregnant, and once the baby comes, she won't be able to do as much around the coffee shop as she does now, so you've decided to help Noah in her place. Obviously, Chrysanthemum follows. She can't very well live on her own."

Nico smirks. "This story makes you two sound completely irresponsible."

Gloria laughs and Kristoff seems affronted. "It does not!"

Nico joins his mother in laughing and pinches his thumb and his index finger together so they're almost touching. "A li'l bit."

Kristoff crosses his arms over his chest, but his mouth is thinning out in the way it always does when he's trying to be serious but wants to smile. "Fine. Fine! This *one time* you can paint us as your ridiculous parents if it helps you bolster your story."

There're so many things Nico could say to help build this. It might be worth having an elven babysitter if he gets to make his father sound ridiculous for once in his life.

Kristoff shakes his head. He doesn't need to be Santa Claus to know Nico's plotting. "But don't go overboard, Nicholas. Someone who hears this story will eventually be part of our family, after all."

"Of course not," Nico says, eyes twinkling with mischief.

NICO DOESN'T UNDERSTAND why he needs Chrysanthemum to join him in this. No matter how much his father said she's there to be a guide, Nico can't believe it's anything other than a rationalization for giving Nico the babysitter he thinks he deserves. It's obvious he doesn't trust him. But what does Kristoff think he will do? Not date anyone the whole year? He's not *that* stubborn.

When Nico complains, in a last-ditch effort to get his father to change his mind, Kristoff is quick to point out Nico's given him no reason to believe he'll take his duty seriously. As such, Kristoff believes it's only fair to have someone there to keep him on track—as a precaution. Nico thinks Noelle would have done a fine enough job, she's definitely got the persistence to annoy him into dating, but his father insists and Nico's learned, after years of butting heads, sometimes it's best to choose his battles. This is definitely not one worth fighting over. Kristoff is far too hell-bent on its importance.

Chrysanthemum's already packed her things so the news of her accompanying them doesn't delay their departure. They leave right as the rest of the house is waking and for some reason, saying goodbye makes his heart pull tight in his chest. It doesn't make sense, but leaving is different somehow. The next time he sees his entire family everything will have changed. Nico doesn't know if he's ready, though. He doesn't think he's ever been ready for any of this, honestly. It's all he can think of on the way to drop Noah and Noelle off at the airport—soon enough he's either going to complete his Santafication or be the first ever heir to fail to do so. He's not sure which he's dreading more. At the moment, they both seem too daunting to handle.

The drive home is much the same, but this time Chrysanthemum has picked up on his mood and tries to distract him. Or at least, she thinks she's distracting him, but in reality, all her questions do is stress him out more. She asks him what his plans are for the year—try his best not to go stir crazy, maybe fall in love. How he intends to find the right man—luck. What he wants from a man—open to myths, not boring, wants kids. How he plans to tell his future partner the family secret—drunk, hopefully with a straight face. It's like being grilled by all of his nieces and nephews at once, but instead of having the attention span of an actual child, Chrysanthemum has unwavering focus. She's unrelenting.

By the time they arrive at Nico's apartment he's ready to crawl into bed and disappear for a while, to turn his brain off and unwind. Instead, he has to pack and most importantly figure out a way to get Chrysanthemum to act more like a real child and not a near seventeen-hundred-year-old being who happens to have the appearance of a child.

"Chrysanthemum, when is your birthday?"

"Hmm. Let me think." She's sitting on the couch cross-legged, eyes squinting in concentration, and though they're only pretending to be siblings, the affection Nico has for her is as real as it is for his actual sisters. She, more than any of the other elves, has been such a calming presence in his life for as long as he can remember. In a lot of ways, she is an older sister to them all. "Well, the Northern Realm was created the day Saint Nicholas died. Then came the Great Flake and the First Snow, and as I was one of the elves born from that snow, I'd say I was born sometime in early December."

"You don't know the exact date?"

Chrysanthemum laughs. "It was a very long time ago, Nicholas. Once you get closer to two thousand than you are to a thousand, dates don't seem to matter anymore. Except Christmas. The elves always remember Christmas."

"Okay, yeah. But as a ten-year-old—which is what you seem like—what you're going to be—you'll need a birthday. When do you want it to be?"

"I'm fond of the number nine."

Nico's been moving around the living room as he talks, assessing what needs to be packed and what he can live without for a year, but he pauses at Chrysanthemum's words, laughing. "You have a favorite number?"

"Yes, it's three. But as the third was too early to be when I was born I figured I'd go with the next best thing."

Nico is curious to know what she is basing her order on, but he doesn't let himself get distracted and pushes on. "December ninth it is then. Next on the agenda..."

Chrysanthemum straightens in her seat, raising an eyebrow at Nico's pause.

He scratches the back of his neck. "What are we going to do about your ears?"

Chrysanthemum smiles, eyes twinkling in a merry sort of way, and Nico watches in awe as her pointed ears start to shrink down, rounding at the edges until they are no different than any other human ones. She touches her fingers to the tips of her ears and glances up at Nico. "How's this?"

He claps his hands together, beaming. "Ahh, fantastic!"

Chrysanthemum's face is transformed by a small but pleased smile. "Anything else?"

Nico mulls it over. They definitely need to figure out their family backstory and other things likely to come up when posing as an elementary school student, but that will take far longer than a few questions, and Nico is mostly blanking on what they'll need to know to be believable, so he sighs. "Yeah, a lot more. But we can talk it over as we pack. I want to leave in the morning. It's a long drive."

Chapter Six

IN THE MORNING, Nico wakes with a headache. He's in desperate need of coffee and ibuprofen, only one of which he has. He went through his cabinets at least seven times in an effort to make coffee magically reappear. What's the point of any of this if he can't make caffeine appear out of thin air?

"I think there's a coffee shop down the corner," Chrysanthemum says.

It startles Nico. "Jesus, Chrys, I forgot you were here!"

"You Hamurişis are so useless without your coffee."

"Too true," Nico concedes, yawning. "Do you want something? Or do you want to join me? It might be nice to stretch your legs before we're stuck in the car all day."

Chrysanthemum considers it for a moment, then shakes her head. "No, I'm going to do a last check of your things to make sure you've gotten everything important."

"That's not necessary," Nico says, but Chrysanthemum doesn't budge. "If you insist...I can bring you something back?"

"Elves don't really do caffeine," she says, and then after a moment she adds, "And as I'm now your run-of-the-mill ten-year-old, I think they don't do coffee either?"

"No," Nico laughs. "They generally don't."

It's a bit weird to leave Chrysanthemum alone, but he has to remind himself as he locks the door she's an immortal being and not actually a child who needs to be watched by him of all people. He's wrapped up in thoughts of how he, Noelle, and Chrysanthemum are going to realistically convince people they are all siblings when he runs headlong into someone else at the coffee shop's door. A warm and sturdy someone.

He has his mouth open to apologize, when he glances up at a familiar set of eyes, and the words catch in his throat.

"Nico?"

It's been nearly seven years since he last saw him, but standing here now, staring at his face pinched in disbelief, the pain is as raw and overwhelming as it did then. Nico doesn't know if he'll ever get over that day, the day he walked away from a boy he cared for, too scared to say I love you, too afraid to tell the truth.

"Taylor," he breathes out.

God, he looks so good.

By the way Taylor's eyes widen, Nico thinks he must have said it out loud. He's blushing, but he can't stop staring. There's so much to look at, so much to take in. He dresses better. He has a beard. His hair is shorter. He's broader now—he must work out more. But his dark brown skin is smooth and unblemished, perfect as ever, and his eyes, those familiar, familiar eyes, are as kind and caring as they were all those years ago. They're the same deep, dark brown Nico could get lost in for days.

He's getting lost in them now. He can't stop staring. Can't get his mouth to form any more words. But neither can Taylor, it seems. They're both standing there, watching each other. And it's weird—it's definitely weird—but it's also nice, in a nostalgic, heart-wrenchingly familiar sort of way.

He doesn't know how long they stand there, watching each other, saying nothing. But the moment is broken when someone pushes past him, grumbling under their breath, "You're blocking the door!"

That's all it takes for them both to come crashing back to reality, and Nico laughs, awkwardly and too loud as Taylor mutters an apology over his shoulder.

They step away from the door at the same time, and Nico is surprised when Taylor says, "It's nice to see you, Nico."

His voice is soft and gentle, and his mouth quirks in a smile that makes the corners of his eyes crinkle and his nose scrunch slightly. Nico can't detect a lie from Taylor which makes Nico's heart hammer against his ribs, embarrassed when the only thing he can think to say is, "I thought you were done with New York."

Taylor laughs, and it's beautiful. Nico wants to hear it again, but he knows it's no longer in the cards for him, not after this moment is over. Taylor rubs a hand over the back of his neck, shrugging, "Yeah, didn't come back for a long time after college."

The unsaid *after you dumped me* hangs heavy in the air, but maybe only for Nico because Taylor keeps talking, smiling easily as he continues, "My sister—you remember Ashley? She's getting married on Saturday. She and her fiancé live here. So, you know."

Ashley had just finished her first year of college the last time he saw Taylor; he can't believe she's getting married. He can't believe Taylor's here, standing in front of him, watching him appraisingly. There're so much he wants to say—I'm sorry, I was an idiot, I hope you're happy now— but the only thing that seems appropriate after so many years is, "That's good. I'm happy for her."

"She's going to freak." Nico's eyes widen against his will, and Taylor barrels on, slight laughter in his voice, "When I tell her I saw you. She's going to go on some shit about serendipity."

Magic finds a way, echoes through his mind, Noelle's voice as real as if she were standing right here with him, smirking as she watches him and Taylor interact.

"Oh, yeah." Nico has to resist the urge to roll his eyes at his own inability to string words together. His tongue feels so thick and his throat so dry he's surprised he's managed any at all so far. "It is—yeah. Quite a coincidence. Us, running into each other right when I'm leaving town."

Taylor smiles, despite the embarrassing way Nico stumbles over his words, a small hint of disappointment radiating off him as he says, "Ah, that's too bad. I would have loved to catch up."

He touches Nico's shoulder, and for a moment, everything seems to slow down. Taylor's mouth is moving, but Nico can only vaguely hear him; all he can focus on is the weight of Taylor's hand, firm and steady on his shoulder and the way it warms him. Then everything's catching up to him, and it's starting to snow, and Taylor's staring at the sky saying, "Huh, I didn't think this was in the forecast."

Nico blinks and Taylor's hand is still on his shoulder. He squeezes it now, laughing, "And you look great too, Nic."

Then his hand is gone and Taylor's giving Nico one last smile before he goes. After, Nico is left standing there in front of the coffee shop dumbfounded because the snow stopped as quickly as it started, and all Nico can think is *that's one hell of a coincidence.*

NICO ARRIVES BACK to the apartment without any coffee and Chrysanthemum doesn't ask why, but he's sure she can pick up on his anxiety. They don't talk for the first hour of the drive. There's a lump in Nico's throat, and his heart is hammering—he can't think of anything other than Taylor.

Two hours in, they stop for coffee, and Chrysanthemum gives him a withering glare, but again, she doesn't actually say anything, and Nico appreciates not having to confront what's on his mind. At least not yet.

They arrive in Pine Cove well after the sun has set. He's riddled with nerves over seeing Taylor, and his legs are jittery from spending the day in the car, but when they turn into Noelle's property, Nico feels lighter already. As they step out of the car, it starts to snow and, for once, it doesn't fill him with dread. But it does make him wonder.

"I didn't think it was supposed to snow today?"

After it started snowing when he saw Taylor, he checked the weather and there was no snow on the forecast for New York City or Pine Cove, yet here he is watching a fresh coat fall over the ground for the second time today.

"It's magic," Chrysanthemum says.

Nico laughs, but he thinks there's truth in what she's said—being here feels good and right. There's a sort of spark, exciting energy filling the air and lifting Nico's spirits as they gather their bags from the trunk. He never used to believe it, because snow is snow, and magic is everywhere, but his mother always used to say *wherever magic is, snow follows,* and now, he wonders if it wasn't just something she said to make him stop complaining when he was younger.

He glances back as Noelle lets them inside and the snow has stopped. Again. Something weird is happening today, and Nico finds himself believing his mother was right, after all. Maybe there is something magical about him being here in this town. Maybe this is a sign that his quest for love isn't doomed for failure. Maybe he should have a little faith. But then, what did it mean earlier when he saw Taylor? Was that some sort of sign as well?

"Nico! Are you even listening to me?"

He's brought out of his thoughts by his sister's borderline aggravated question. "Sorry, I didn't hear you. I was thinking—"

He stops short. He doesn't know how to vocalize the mix of emotions warring inside him. There's a soothing presence to Pine Cove making him feel infinitely calmer about what's to come, but there's also this niggling sensation at the back of his mind telling him the start-and-stop snow can't merely be a coincidence. He knows something strange is going on, but he can't tell what. Then there's the lump lodged in his throat—the one he's had since he left Taylor—which acts as a physical reminder of all the things he left unsaid. He'd frozen and let Taylor walk away without expressing years of regret as he wanted to. As he should have.

Noelle purses her lips, eyes narrowing. "What's up with you?"

Chrysanthemum snorts. "I've been trying to figure that out all day."

Noelle's eyebrows shoot up, and she nearly coos in excitement. "You're keeping a secret! Come on, tell us!"

"Your house is nice," he says pushing past her and heading for the living room.

"You're deflecting."

"I remember it being smaller? Did you remodel?"

He's sinking into the couch, hoping she'll drop it, and is shocked when she gives him a pointed frown but engages with the subject change, anyway. "No, it's the same as always. But you were such an ass last time and thought you were suffocating in small-town isolation. What was it you said when visited before?"

Nico's cheeks burn. "I don't know what you're talking about."

"Ah," Noelle says, feigning an epiphany. "I remember it now. You said, 'If I wanted to be isolated from the world, I'd visit home more often' and yet here you are. Smiling. In my tiny town. Pretending you love it to avoid talking."

Chrysanthemum is perched on the arm of the couch, watching him as expectantly as Noelle, and Nico crumbles.

"Fine! Fine! I compliment your house, which is nice by the way, but all you want to hear about is my awkward run-in with my ex! Fine!"

Chrysanthemum's mouth twists in sympathy while Noelle squeals. "Who? Where? Nico, tell me everything!"

Nico is saved by Noah entering the room, kind voice full of laughter as he says, "Honey, he's just gotten here, and you're already interrogating him?"

"Obviously," Nico says, only slightly bitter, and Noelle waves a hand in the air, dismissing them both.

"Noah, he ran into an ex! I don't know anything about his exes, and frankly, I'm not even sure I knew he had any until this moment in time. So I obviously need to hear all about him in order to see if I was right about my assessment of Elliott."

Noah breathes out a huff of laughter at the same time Nico asks, "Who's Elliott?"

Noelle throws her hands in the air, very nearly snapping. "Do you even listen when I speak to you, Nico? He's the man I told you about! The one who lives above the coffee shop?"

"Oh, right. I thought his name was Evan."

Chrysanthemum laughs and Noah shrugs. "At least he got the E right?"

"He's supposed to be good with names!"

"I am good with names!"

"Ha! You admit you weren't listening, then."

Noah holds his hands up, stopping them. "While I would love to watch you two chew each other's ears off...dinner is ready."

Noelle deflates and points a finger at Nico, leveling him with a sharp look. "Fine. But don't think this means you've gotten out of telling me about your ex. I want to hear all about it over dinner."

"Fine," Nico groans.

He wants to be difficult and refuse to talk, but sitting at the table with the three of them soothes him, taking the fight right out of him. It's always been easy to talk to Noelle, no matter how hard he tried to keep things to himself over the years, and he ends up saying, after the food is passed around and the quiet has stretched on long enough to be uncomfortable, "Do you remember Taylor? My roommate in college?"

"Yeah but..." Understanding dawns on her before she finishes her thought, and her eyes go impossibly wide. She presses a hand to her mouth for a brief moment before changing gears. "He's the ex?"

"Yeah."

"The whole time?"

"No, no. Nothing official until senior year."

Noelle arches an eyebrow and Nico blushes. "Shut up! You know how college is—we didn't—it wasn't—it wasn't serious until that last year."

Noelle nods and waits for him to continue, and when he doesn't, she prompts, "I assume he's who you ran into today?"

"Yeah," Nico swallows hard, the overwhelming regret clawing at his chest again.

Chrysanthemum speaks this time, calm and understanding, "By the way you've been acting since you came back with no coffee, I presume you ran into him there?"

Nico nods and Noah chimes in, his voice low and sympathetic, "And I'm going to assume since you look like we're pulling teeth here, it didn't end very well."

Nico laughs, even though it pains him to say, "You'd be correct there."

"Who's fault?"

Nico prickles. "Mine obviously."

Noelle glances toward her husband, and then her eyes narrow on Nico, and she purses her lips. "No, it actually isn't obvious at all by how forlorn you look. Seems he did a number on your heart."

Nico scrapes a hand over his face, failing miserably at staving off the familiar rush of shame building up in his gut. The words are small and vulnerable, even to his own ears. "Is he the one who got away if I pushed him out the door?"

"Ah," Noelle says, not sounding nearly as sympathetic as he'd prefer. "Self-sabotaging your love life isn't a new thing then."

Nico wants to disagree, but he has no leg to stand on at all. It's been like this since the moment he broke it off with Taylor. "Yeah," he shrugs. "I guess he was the start of it all."

Noelle gives him a long, appraising look, and then quirks her head to the side. "Now, now, my little Tico. Don't give yourself too much credit! Dad's got more to do with this shit you carry around than you'd care to admit."

"Noelle," Noah says reproachfully.

She crosses her arms, leans back in her seat, and huffs, "What? We all know he's the cause!"

She turns her attention back to Nico, and while her eyes are softer now, her voice is fierce. "Look Nic, Dad's put a lot of pressure on you which sucks, but— shit. This isn't about him. This is about you and your happiness and self-sabotaging ends *now*."

His focus shifts around the table. Noah appears a little wary, but Nico can sense he believes his wife to be right, and Chrysanthemum assesses him with a careful expression, raising an eyebrow when Nico's gaze lands on her.

"And what do you think, Chrys?"

She stares at him for a long moment, saying nothing, and then finally, when Nico can't stand the quiet any longer, she speaks, "I think you need to consider, above all else, what it is you want for your own life."

"I want—"

The words get caught in his throat, and he has to avert his eyes, no longer able to hold the gaze of Chrysanthemum. He peers at the table, nervously fiddling with his hands, and mumbles, "I want to be happy without worrying I'll disappoint the family legacy."

"What will make you happy?"

Chrysanthemum's voice is gentle and reaffirming, and Nico looks up, much more confident with the conclusion he's come to than he was the moment before. "I want to fall in love and get married and have a family and be happy."

Chrysanthemum smiles and the tension eases out of Nico's shoulders. He smiles when Noelle says, "Then that's what you focus on, no more thinking about becoming Santa Claus. No more worrying about what Dad will think. You're here away from all that, and all you need to focus on is you and love and finding a nice guy who makes you happy."

Even though he knows it's not that easy, and no amount of posturing is going to eliminate his anxiety surrounding the year running out, in this moment, he knows Noelle is right. All he has to concern himself with is finding someone who makes him happy. Nothing else matters.

Chapter Seven

NICO SPENDS HIS first two days in Pine Cove setting up his and Chrysanthemum's space in Noelle's home. It doesn't take long. He didn't bring very much, and Chrysanthemum brought even less. Chrysanthemum takes the guest room in the main house and Nico sets himself up in the apartment above their garage. If anyone notices he draws the process out, they don't question it. Noelle doesn't lose her patience with how he's clearly avoiding going out and exploring Pine Cove until dinner on New Year's Eve.

Noah is clearing the plates from the table, insisting he doesn't need Nico's help, and Noelle steeples her fingers in front of her mouth and gives him a hard look. "Nico, Nico, Nico."

"Yes, Noelle," Nico says, gearing up for confrontation. He knows the triple name is always a sign Noelle has something on her mind.

"Are you going to sit here all night and avoid putting yourself out there, or are you going to go out and meet people and celebrate New Year's?"

Nico laughs. "Straight to the point as always! I do appreciate that you don't beat around the bush."

Noelle's eyes narrow. "You're deflecting."

"I'm not!" Nico protests, but he doesn't have much fight in him. Noelle knows him far too well to pretend he's not been hiding away in his room because meeting people makes him nervous. Coming to a tiny town with a limited population, and probably an even smaller number of queer men to meet, seemed like a bad idea the moment he was far enough removed from his father's concerns over the very same thing to see past his own spite. He shrugs, mouth turned down in a frown. "I'd go out but uh...where?"

Noelle beams at him. She must have expected him to put up more of a fight. However, staying in and hiding has done nothing but make him antsy. If he's honest, the appeal of getting out and doing something—anything at all—far outweighs any anxiety he may have.

"Well since you asked..." Noelle says with a satisfied lilt to her voice.

Noah comes back then, shakes his head as he sits down at the table again, and laughs, "Noelle, honey, you didn't give him any other choice but to ask."

Chrysanthemum laughs into her hand, and Nico smiles, amused by the way Noelle waves Noah's comments off, continuing on as if she was never interrupted. "I think you should go down to Winnie's. The bar on Main Street is super popular and I think you'll love it there."

"Any particular reason?"

"Well for starters, Winnie is the sweetest, and her wife—"

"Her wife?"

"Yes, her wife, Jan, makes an amazing cocktail."

Knowing there's a popular bar in this town owned by lesbians calms his nerves almost instantly. He doesn't need any more convincing, but he still asks, "Anything else?"

Noelle's face twists with a sly smile. Nico's stomach drops, and his heartbeat quickens as she says, "It's a known hangout for that guy I told you about. Maybe he'll be there."

"You had me, and then you lost me," he says, throat tight.

Noelle throws her hands in the air, but Chrysanthemum speaks first, her voice calm and soothing, "Nicholas, you won't be able to find love how you want if you never put yourself out there. You owe it to yourself to have a little fun, to see where it takes you."

He turns to Noah, seeking some sort of solidarity, but he gives him a small shrug, mouth titled up in a small smile, "I think it'll be good for you, man. You seem stressed."

"Fine!" He says. As he gets up, the chair scrapes harshly against the floor; the sound is grating and makes him flinch. His shoulders slump, and he mumbles, "Sorry for snapping. I know you're all just trying to be supportive and encouraging, but I'm nervous and a little out of my depth and I..."

He doesn't know how to finish the sentence; he only knows he's overwhelmed, but Noelle smiles up at him sympathetically and says, "Oh Tico, what did we say when you got here? No more self-sabotage! Don't think of this as a foray into dating. Just go out and have fun! Meet some people and celebrate the New Year! Act how you would any other time without wondering what you're supposed to be doing or what you think you're already supposed to have accomplished. Fuck all that! Go have fun!"

Nico laughs and stares at Noelle in disbelief. "You make it sound so much easier than it actually is."

Before she can argue, he adds, "And don't think you're fooling anyone here with how hard you're trying to get me to go out. You're obviously living vicariously through me."

Noelle scoffs and Noah laughs, voice beyond fond as he says, "You do love New Year's Eve cocktails."

"Too true," Noelle concedes. "You'll have to have one of Jan's New Year's drinks. She's always making something original and most of the time they're excellent." She grimaces, nose wrinkling up in disgust as she remembers something. "Though, there was the one from 2012…"

"You sure know how to talk someone up. I'm brimming with confidence in her ability."

"Oh shut up! Everyone has an off day!"

Nico shrugs and finally leaves the kitchen, turning back at the last minute to ask, "Chrys, are you fine with me going out?"

Chrysanthemum doesn't roll her eyes, but her tone says it's probably a very near thing. "Nicholas, you don't actually have to take care of me. Plus, you're only trying to find reasons to stay in at this point."

He wants to disagree, but Chrysanthemum arches an eyebrow at him, and he knows better than to try to lie to her. "All right, if you all insist. I'll go out and have some *fun*."

IT TAKES HIM far longer to get ready than it should, or ever normally would, because Noelle insists on approving his outfit. She's more excited he's going out than he is, and he doesn't have the heart to be a dick to her, no matter how much he wants to tell her to stop mothering him.

The walk to Winnie's isn't long, but he doubts anything in Pine Cove is, and he's honestly surprised to see the turnout. He had expected there to be a small gathering, but instead, he opens the door to a raucous blend of music and laughter and a bar full of people. He'd been nervous he'd feel exposed, too noticeable in a barely crowded place, but this is an environment he's used to. This is the type of place he loves. Places he can slip into and not be overwhelmed by the pinpoint accuracy of picking up on individual emotions. Instead, it's warm vibrating energy coursing through him all at once. It's invigorating. Noelle was right to push him out of the house. He's been here for less than a minute, and he already feels better than he has in weeks.

He makes his way to the bar, not surprised in the slightest to find Dick Clark's Rockin' New Year's Eve muted on the television mounted to the wall behind, and waits until he can place his order. It doesn't take too long, and when the bartender finally sets her sight on him, he's taken aback by how kind her face is and the positive energy radiating off her. She's short and round and there're laugh lines at the corners of her mouth and eyes. She has short gray hair and golden skin, and when she smiles at him, Nico's calmer than he's ever felt before. He wonders, for a moment, if soothing has anything to do with her power but shakes off the thought, knowing he'll probably never find out.

"What can I get you, sweetheart?"

"I've been told to get Jan's New Year's special."

Her eyes light up at the mention of Jan, and he decides this must be Winnie because he can sense the warmth of love coming off her.

"It's a treat this year," she says as she makes him a bright-blue drink, and he wishes Noelle was here with him. What is it she always used to say to him when they'd go out together? *The brighter the drink, the drunker you get.* He takes a sip of the cocktail and laughs into his glass because it is strong, but he's sure Noelle's catchphrase from her twenties had absolutely nothing to do with the content of the drinks and everything to do with her inability to not order every single one of them. The drink is good, and the bar is loud and energetic, but he still wishes Noelle was here with him. She always knows how to make him enjoy the moment, to forget his worries, and just live. Even with the alcohol and Winnie's smile and the drunken excitement of the bar's patrons coursing through and putting him at ease, he still craves the security Noelle provides.

He's finishing his second drink and considering another when a hand touches his elbow. It's deliberate and intentional, someone trying to get his attention. He turns in his seat and there's a beautiful woman staring up at him. She has pale brown skin, straight black hair, and beautiful brown eyes. She's short, with wide hips, and when she talks her voice carries over the noise of the bar. "You're new here."

It's not a question, but she seems to expect a confirmation, and Nico's nerves flare up again. He hates this part of small towns. He's close to stumbling his way through an answer when a tall man sidles up behind her. He places a large hand on her shoulder and squeezes gently. "Eliza, don't scare the new guy off before we've even learned his name."

His voice doesn't travel over the sound around them as well as Eliza's did, but Nico can hear the laughter as he speaks and see the way his face transforms with charming warmth. His pale, freckly skin is flushed pink over his cheeks and nose, and his eyes are shining bright in the dull light of the bar. He has dark, curly brown hair and more than a day's worth of stubble on his jaw, and Nico's breath catches in his throat—he's beautiful.

He leans down and sets his chin on the top of Eliza's head and gives Nico a small, almost shy smile, and Eliza huffs out a laugh, leaning into the guy's touch. "All right, all right, all right." Her face softens and she turns her attention back to Nico. "What's your name then, handsome?"

Maybe it's the alcohol or maybe it's the way this guy is looking at him, unblinking green eyes staring back at him expectantly, but the words fall out of his mouth before he can rethink his response. "I'm gay."

There's a split second before his brain catches up with his mouth where Nico watches as Eliza's smile grows, and she leans farther back against the guy behind her. She tilts her head up to whisper in his ear, and then Nico realizes what he's said. His face burns in embarrassment, and his eyes widen in shock. "Oh, Jesus."

Eliza straightens up and offers Nico her hand. "Well, I'm bi! Usually I introduce myself and get to know someone before offering it up, but I admire your forwardness. I'm Eliza by the way, but you already heard Elly-belly here call me that."

Nico takes her hand and mumbles an apology, but neither she nor the guy behind her seems too bothered by his abrupt confession, so he tries not to be too embarrassed. "I'm Nico. I, uh, definitely don't usually introduce myself as gay. Hopefully, I'll be leaving that behind with the rest of this year."

Elly-belly, which can't possibly be his real name, is smiling at him again. It's still a little shy, but it's broader this time, dazzling in the way it lights up his face, and Nico is once again taken aback by how pretty he is. Nico's staring—he knows he is—but he can't make himself look away, no matter how hot his face burns in embarrassment. He's not been so instantly mesmerized by someone since Taylor, and Nico wonders if that's because he's closed himself off to this sort of emotion or if it means anything special. He doesn't believe in signs, but if he did, this might be one.

Elly-belly extends his hand out around Eliza. His arm brushes against her side as he reaches for Nico's, and he wonders, with the way they keep touching, if they're together. His thought is cut short when Elly-belly says, "I'm bi, but people usually just call me Elliot."

He pulls his hand away, mouth slanting up at the corners, and he squeezes Eliza's shoulder. "Or if you're Eliza, you call me increasingly more ridiculous names in an effort to embarrass me in public. Though, I do prefer Elliott."

His name sounds familiar, but Nico can't place it over the ringing in his ears and the fluttering in his stomach that started the moment Elliott said he was bi.

"Well," Nico says, deliberately playful in an attempt to mask the way his mouth dries as Elliott curls back against Eliza, "since we're all queer here, I guess we have to be friends now."

Elliot's eyes sparkle with the force of his laughter and Eliza's mouth curls up in a grin. "Oh Nico, I like you. I think we're going get along quite well."

After their laughter dies down, they welcome him in as if it's nothing, like he's not the new guy in town they've only just met, as if they've known him for longer than ten minutes. Eliza orders the next round of drinks, tequila shots and Jan's New Year's special as a chaser, and then she ushers him and Elliot to a booth at the back of the bar. He spends the dwindling hours of 2017 there, bracketed between Eliza and Elliot, drinking and laughing, and a light sort of ease builds in his chest as he finally allows himself to have a good time.

As the bar starts counting down to midnight, Eliza leans forward to talk around Nico, asking Elliot, "You want to be my first kiss of the New Year?"

Elliot's sitting so close Nico can feel him lean forward and jealousy curls tight in Nico's chest when he reaches around and kisses Eliza as the countdown concludes. It's over in an instant, quick and chaste, and they're both laughing as they pull away, and then Eliza's off, pushing into the crowd of the bar to celebrate the New Year with everyone else. His inhibitions are gone, with how much he's had to drink, and the desperation of wanting Elliott to be single wins out. He's ready to ask if they're a thing, if Elliott's unavailable, when Elliot looks to him and the question gets lost on the tip of his tongue. Elliot's settled in at Nico's side again, and the minimal space between them from before is now completely gone as Elliott twists in his seat, shifting even closer. He places a large hand on Nico's neck, his thumb brushing Nico's jaw, and raises an eyebrow as he leans forward slightly, asking without saying, and Nico shrugs, meeting him the rest of the way.

Elliott's mouth is warm and inviting. Nico expects it to be over as quickly as his and Eliza's kiss had been, but then Elliott's hand is curling around the back of his neck, fingers brushing against the hairs at the base of his skull, pulling him in closer. Elliott licks into Nico's mouth, eliciting a soft sigh from Nico, and Nico's pleased when Elliot's mouth twists up in a smile against his own. They stay there, wrapped in each other's kisses for a long moment, until Elliot eventually pulls away, touching the pads of his fingers to his reddened lips. Nico wants to take him home; that much he knows, but he also doesn't want to ruin a potential friendship with the first two people his age he's met in Pine Cove by having a one-night stand.

Elliot smiles, eyes twinkling. "It was nice to meet you, Nico. Happy New Year."

Nico breathes out, mouth twitching in a smile of his own, "Yeah, you too."

Chapter Eight

HE SPENDS THE next morning hungover, lights turned off and curtains shut. He'd be absolutely miserable if it weren't for the warmth growing larger in his chest every time he thinks of Elliott. His only regret from the night before is forgetting to get Elliott's number, but he expects, or at least he hopes, in a town the size of Pine Cove it won't take too long to run into him again. What he's not expecting is to be brought face-to-face with him the evening after their kiss when he drags himself out into the real world.

In an unsurprising turn of luck, he runs right into Elliott at Noelle's coffee shop after deciding to go out in too-big glasses and a ratty old college sweater.

"I've got to stop doing this," he mumbles under his breath.

"Oh, you make a habit of bumping into people too? We really are going to get along then. Eliza will have someone else to tease for being clumsy."

"Elliott?" Nico asks, admittedly not his best response, but he's got a lingering headache, so he gives himself a pass.

"In the flesh," Elliott smiles and Nico does too. This is okay. He can do this. He knows how to talk to people sober.

"I didn't expect to see you here but...uh. Yeah, I'm glad I ran into you. I meant to get your number last night but. You know. That didn't happen."

God, you're nailing it here, Nico. Elliot doesn't seem to mind Nico's blundering, though, smile only growing.

"Yeah, I actually live upstairs."

Wait. No. What? This can't be right. "The g— You're Elliott?"

Elliott's nose scrunches up and his eyebrows knit together. "Yes, we just went over this."

His perplexed expression and the barely veiled amusement in his tone would be adorable if Nico wasn't finally starting to put two and two together.

"Uh, sorry. My sister," he gestures around the coffee shop. "She owns this place, and she might've mentioned you. I didn't—"

"Make the connection last night?"

Nico's face is burning, and he hopes it's not as noticeable as it feels. "In my defense, Elliot's not exactly an *uncommon* name."

Elliott tilts his head to the side, a faint smile still playing at his lips, and Nico scrubs a hand over his face, pushing his glasses out of the way to pinch the bridge of his nose. "And honestly, I'm terrible at listening to my sister when she's trying to set me up."

"Hmm." Elliott purses his lips and then he's laughing. "I think it's probably for the best you didn't make the connection. Our meeting was a lot more enjoyable than a setup."

"Oh, yeah," Nico says, surprised. And honestly, has he always been this out of his depth talking to men? He can't remember ever being this bad, but Elliot's making him tongue-tied and nervous in a way he hasn't been since he was a teenager and not yet fully embracing his attraction to men.

"If you want, if your sister thinking I'm a good match doesn't turn you off—I know I hate when Eliza tries to set me up with people—we could still exchange numbers?"

There's a hint of shyness, maybe even slight concern, in his voice, putting Nico at ease; at least, he's not the only one bridled with nerves here. He digs his phone out of his pocket and holds his hand out, offering it up. "Yeah, yeah. I'd love that, actually."

ON TUESDAY, NICO starts at Kahveci's, where he's trained by the seventeen-year-old barista named Addison, who has dark-brown skin, round glasses, and a large Afro she's tucked a flower into above her right ear. She's funny and sarcastic and makes Nico laugh with how blunt she can be when he messes up.

On Wednesday, Nico takes Chrysanthemum to Pine Cove Elementary and gets her squared away for starting school the next day. She doesn't seem pleased in the slightest at the idea of spending her days surrounded by actual ten-year-olds, learning things she grasped over a thousand years ago, but she puts on a smile and plays the part of a nervous fourth-grade transfer student easily. Nico spends the entire time filling out paperwork, wondering how long it will take them to convince his father this charade is, at best, unnecessary and, at worst, counterproductive.

On Thursday, Chrysanthemum starts school, and Elliot texts him to see if he wants to hang out on Saturday. It takes Nico three hours to text back a yes, and by the time he goes to bed, he feels like a bumbling teenager with a crush all over again.

On Friday, Nico spends his entire shift overthinking the next day. He messes up three whole drinks before Addison takes pity on him and puts him at the cash register. She waits until they're closing to tease him about being too old to get this nervous over a date. Addison rolls her eyes as he insists it's not a date, even though he hopes it is.

On Saturday, he spends the entire morning planning what to wear to hang out with Elliott only to rethink it at the very last minute and change completely. He meets Elliot at Kahveci's a few minutes after seven. He's waiting right inside the store, a to-go cup in each hand, not paying attention as Nico walks through the door. Elliott startles as Nico cups his hand under his elbow to get his attention.

"Sorry, didn't mean to scare you. Or be late but…" He shrugs, thinking better of divulging how long it took him to get ready. He doesn't need to make himself feel any more ridiculous than he already does.

Elliott smiles, though, and a little of Nico's nerves melt away. Elliott pushes one of the drinks into Nico's hands and gestures to the door with the other. "It's not a problem. This may come as a surprise, I know. My students think I'm quite intimidating, but I'm actually just a big, jumpy man who scares far too easily for his own good."

Nico laughs into his cup, sipping at the hot chocolate, before sweeping his gaze over Elliot, deadpanning. "Ah yeah, very intimidating demeanor for sure."

Elliott shrugs, a small smile tugging at the corner of his lips. "By fourth grade standards, at least. I think it might be the height. Though, I have been told by a fifth grader I'm basically Gumby so who knows? Summer changes them."

"You teach fourth grade?" Nico asks, stomach bubbling uncomfortably at the idea of him being Chrysanthemum's teacher. There's got to be more than one, right? Or is this town too small? Should he ask? Or would that make things weird?

"Yeah, me and Eliza are," Elliott says and Nico's heart stutters with hope—maybe Eliza is her teacher. Before he can ask Elliot if Chrysanthemum is in his class, it starts to snow.

Nico does his best not to roll his eyes but internally groans as Elliott says, "Oh, that's weird. No snow in the forecast."

Why does this keep happening?

Elliott assesses him, eyes lingering on the pull of his Henley over his shoulders for a moment, and then he shakes his head and clears his throat. "Aren't you cold?"

"Nope, I never get cold."

Elliott considers him for a moment, doubt written across his face, and then his face erupts in a broad smile. "How useful. Especially for tonight. I thought we'd walk through town and enjoy all the lights before they get taken down."

In most circumstances, he'd think the idea was awful—he spends so much time wrapped up in Christmas he'd prefer not to spend his spare time dwelling on it. For a split second, he contemplates saying something, telling Elliott he'd rather not. Elliott looks hopeful, and there's an excitement coursing through Nico not entirely his own, and he decides against refusing the offer. He knows this feeling, absorbing and experiencing other people's emotions when they're near is as common as breathing for him, but usually it's fleeting, gone an instant after he's been able to parse what they're feeling. But this one stays, the excitement filling him with a bubble of warmth as he lets Elliott lead the way, taking him through town to see the remaining holiday decorations.

It's fun and Nico is delighted by Elliott's company. Their hands brush, sending a shock up his arm. Elliott glances back at him right as flurries start to fall around them again. One lands on his nose, and his face scrunches up with the cold and bemusement. "The weather's been very strange tonight."

"Ha. Yeah," Nico says, the suspicion he may be the cause growing with every weird instance of start-and-stop snow he experiences. He'll have to ask someone—this can't be a coincidence.

Elliott gives him an odd look, almost like he wants to ask something but thinks better of it, and it's all too familiar. This happens a lot in a world full of magic, especially when weird things start happening. Everyone wants to ask *is this your magic* but knows it's too forward, too brazen, especially of someone you barely know. So they don't; they bury the curiosity and move forward like it's nothing. Nico's always thought it's a social taboo they should have gotten over by now, but then all these weird things keep happening around him, and Nico's relieved Elliott's not asking. He doesn't want to explain, not when there's a chance he wouldn't be believed anyway.

He pushes the nerves away and lets himself get lost in the moment with Elliott instead. They've only just met. There's no need to worry himself with broaching such an intimate subject yet, not when he doesn't know if this is going anywhere.

They kissed on New Year's Eve, but Nico's kissed plenty of people to know it doesn't always mean anything. Elliott also kissed Eliza—Nico's stomach still twists uncomfortably at the thought— and it was New Year's Eve, after all. People do that. They kiss people on New Year's Eve, and it doesn't have to mean something. Nico knows that. He tamps down his desire and tries to focus on getting to know Elliott. He and Eliza are the only two people other than his family and Chrysanthemum he knows in this town, and he'd regret ruining a budding friendship by making a move too soon— and by god, does he want to kiss Elliott again.

As the night ends, Elliott walks him all the way back to Noelle's house and the burning question of whether this is headed anywhere more than friendship is answered without Nico's prompting.

"So, I was thinking..." Elliott says as Nico unlocks the front door.

Nico glances back at him, hand still on the doorknob. Elliott is biting his lip, examining his shoes, shoulders hunched in a shy, nervous sort of way. Elliott's shift in demeanor makes Nico's stomach flip.

He's not known him long, but Nico is already hopelessly endeared by how much Elliott slips between shy and confident, depending on the situation. When Elliott doesn't say anything, though, Nico prompts him. "So you were thinking?"

Elliott's gaze darts up, eyes wide and cheeks flushed pink, the cold obviously affecting him. "Oh, yes. Um. Well."

He's shuffling his feet, fidgeting with the hem of his sweater. "Well. This was fun, and I was thinking, if you want to, of course, we could go to dinner next Saturday."

"Like a date?" He tries to keep the hope out of his voice—he doesn't want to sound too eager—but it's what he wants it to be.

"Yeah," Elliott says. He seems nervous and Nico is so happy they're on the same page his answer comes out too loud.

He'd be embarrassed, but Elliott's smile radiates in the soft porch light when Nico says yes again, calmer this time, and Nico knows it doesn't matter. They have a date and they're both happy about it—there's no use hiding it.

Chapter Nine

THE HIGH HE has from scheduling a date with someone he wants a second one with doesn't last long. Chrysanthemum comes home from school on Thursday with a wary quality to her eyes and a small frown, and Nico knows something's up.

"What's the matter?"

"My teacher wants to have a conference with you," she says matter-of-factly, and Nico grimaces.

"Okay, well. I guess as I'm your acting guardian that's to be expected. When?"

"Tomorrow after school ends. If you're available."

"I am," he confirms. Her face doesn't change; she's watching him very carefully, and Nico can tell she's keeping information from him. She's nervous in a way he has never seen or felt from her. "What's wrong?"

She purses her lips and lets out an exasperated puff of air. "I didn't know how to tell you this, but my teacher is the man you like."

Nico's heart plummets, hands clamming up with his unease as Chrysanthemum voices what's been worrying him since he found out Elliott taught fourth grade.

"I don't know how this will affect your blossoming romance, Nicholas. But I do not think your father thought this plan out well enough. He made a rash decision fueled by his desire to keep an eye on you, to soothe his own concerns over the deadline, without thinking through how this could complicate things."

Nico blinks back at her, unsure of what to say. There's a surge of fierce disappointment radiating from her, and Nico is taken aback, speechless. It would be nice to have her on his side in this if it weren't for how desperate he was for this not to complicate things. For once in his entire life, he'd prefer for his father to be right than have this thing with Elliott go up in flames before it ever even started.

Nico rubs a hand over his face and groans, "This sucks."

Chrysanthemum gives him a small smile before walking off, adding at the last moment, "I do hope it doesn't complicate things. You seem quite smitten."

"Yeah," he mumbles as she walks off. He really, truly is.

NICO SHOULD HAVE known meeting someone he was interested in days after moving to town was too good to be true. He should have known there was no way this happiness building up inside could last. He should have braced himself for bitter disappointment accompanying yet another bump in the road to love popping up, even if it was completely out of his control. For once.

He should have expected to not have things be smooth sailing once he finally got on board with falling in love. It's how things go, right? When he walks into the classroom with *Mr. Laska* on a little plaque to the right of the door, he's crushed to see the way Elliott's face pales, and his mouth drops open in shock as he recognizes Nico. This can't be a good sign.

"Nico?"

Nico tries to smile, but he's sure it comes across as a grimace. "Yeah."

Elliott starts to stand and then sits back at his desk. A flash of frustration washes over Nico, which makes his stomach swoop uncomfortably as Elliott asks, surprised, "Chrysanthemum is *your daughter?*"

Nico can tell he's upset, with or without his powers, and the added layer of knowing isn't a pleasant experience. He never wanted this. He knew his father's plan was going to bite him in the ass. Despite knowing this, he can't seem to direct any of his anger at his father; it's only pointed inward. He knew bringing Chrysanthemum along for this quest would end badly, yet he barely put up any fight at all, and now he was going to pay for it.

"No," he says, sitting in the chair on the other side of Elliott's desk. "She's not my daughter."

Elliott's relieved and Nico revels in the way it washes over him, calming his nerves for a moment. Elliott quirks an eyebrow at him, though, and Nico doesn't know how to explain the situation with anything but the truth. It can't hurt to be upfront from the get-go. Managing Elliott's reaction to being Santa's son may be easier if he has time to prove it, instead of being preoccupied with what Chrysanthemum being in his class will mean for them.

"Would you believe me if I told you she's my elf supervisor, and I'm the son of Santa Claus?"

Elliott blinks back at him, stunned. His escaping laugh does nothing to dampen Nico's growing anxiety and Nico wishes he was surprised when Elliott says, "No, I wouldn't."

"Hm, I didn't think you would," Nico says, deflating. Elliott's staring back at him, mouth twitching in a small smile, and Nico wants to scream. It wasn't supposed to be this hard. It could have been fine if his father had only trusted him. Instead, he's sitting in a too-small children's chair, getting told by the guy he's interested in his reality isn't believable. It's a great start to the weekend. "Well, since you're not buying she's an elf, let's say she's my sister."

Nico watches as Elliott's face falls. The glimmer of relief he experienced moments before is forcibly yanked from his chest, replaced by a cold disappointment seeping through his body and settling in the pit of his stomach. The feeling is as much Elliott's as it is his own and before Elliott can say anything, Nico adds, "Honestly, I didn't realize you might be her teacher until last Saturday. I mean, how could I? I didn't know you were a teacher! But then I was too afraid to ask because I didn't know how you'd react." He grimaces, gesturing wildly. "Which it seems I was right to be. Anyway, Chrys came home yesterday and told me, and I could've texted you, but I thought having this conversation in person would be better. I don't know. It doesn't have to be weird. Is it weird? I hope it's not weird."

Elliott considers him for a long moment. His emotions are too mottled up to decipher; they rush from Elliott rapidly, crashing into Nico with such force he can't even begin to parse the specifics. Then finally, Elliott answers, "It's not weird. I mean, it's a small town. I've had several students in my class related to people I know."

Nico sighs in relief; maybe Kristoff hasn't messed everything up. The relief lasts a heartbeat before Elliott is crushing all hope he had for this working out by saying, "Unfortunately, I think it'd be highly unprofessional of me to date the brother of one of my students."

Nico slumps in his chair. "I thought you might say that. So I guess dinner's off tomorrow?"

"Yeah, I guess so," Elliott says, mouth turned down in a frown, eyes darting quickly around the room. Elliott's sadness and disappointment curl in Nico's stomach, but he has enough of that to go around for both of them—he doesn't need Elliott's mingling with his own.

"Would've been nice if you had believed I'm the heir to Santa's sleigh."

Elliott laughs, eyes twinkling as they meet his own once again, and Nico thinks that's worth it, at least. "Probably would be but"—he shrugs—"I think I'd know if Santa Claus was actually real."

Elliott's certainty is why he never told Taylor and why he closed himself off to finding love all these years. A searing hot resentment coils around his heart and makes him hate the hand he's been dealt even more. No one—not even people full of magic of their own—can believe Santa Claus is anything other than a silly, little children's story. Elliott thinks he's joking, and Nico can't imagine how awful this would be if he actually intended for Elliott to believe him.

He manages—but barely—to get through the rest of their meeting without showing how upset he is and mentally pats himself on the back when he doesn't snap back, *Yes, because she's a fucking immortal elf,* when Elliott asks if Chrysanthemum has always been so peculiar. Instead, he laughs it off and tells him it's the result of being adopted into a family of five adult siblings. Elliott buys it, and Nico's impressed with his own ability to lie so believably on the fly. Especially when Elliott asks, voice timid, "I don't mean to pry, but it'll help me to get an understanding of her, but uh, did something happen to your parents for you to be her guardian?"

Trepidation is emitting from Elliott, and Nico's eyes go wide on their own accord. He laughs, but he tries to turn it into a cough. "Oh, god, no. No! They've decided to take a year-long vacation from their toy empire. So Chrys is with me while I help out around Kahveci's since Noelle is having a baby. Which is also why I'm the guardian on paper even though Noah and Noelle are doing as much parenting in this whole thing as I am. It's a joint effort, but I didn't want to add more stress to their lives by making them come to school meetings and such. "

Elliott gives off a quick pulse of affection as Nico explains how he's taken on more responsibility in order to help Noelle, but it's quickly drowned out by shock. Elliott's eyes widen, and Nico answers the question he senses Elliott is too polite to ask. "Yeah, it was a quite a rash decision. Chrys wanted to go with them. She got it in her head a private tutor would be amazing while going abroad with them, but our dad thinks it'll be good for her to have the structure of an actual school."

He shrugs; the reasoning definitely sounds like Kristoff. "I don't know how long it'll last, though. My mom's going to miss her like crazy."

Elliott's face doesn't show it, but there's a very fleeting bit of hope coming off him after Nico admits his mother will miss Chrysanthemum. Nico tries to stamp it out before it takes hold in him, too, but it's futile. He noticed it earlier, but it's even more obvious now: Elliott's emotions linger inside Nico in a way one else's ever have. Despite knowing Kristoff is too stubborn to be talked into pulling Chrysanthemum out of this charade, Nico can't shake the hope Elliott's imbibed in him—no matter how hard he tries.

He entertains the idea of Chrysanthemum leaving Pine Cove the entire walk home. Then he lets out a frustrated growl and bangs his head against the front door before going inside.

"What's wrong with you?" Noelle asks as he walks into the kitchen and slumps against the island countertop, resting his head in the crook of his elbow.

He groans, not even making her wait as he usually would. He peeks over his arm and shrugs, absolutely defeated. "Oh, you know how it goes: get excited for a date, find out he's your fake sister's teacher, date gets canceled for the sake of professionalism."

"No. *No.* No. You've got to be kidding me, right?"

She sounds furious and Nico sighs. "I wish I was. But no, good ol' Kristoff has gone and fucked everything up for me before I could do it myself."

"You have to call him! Tell him what he's done. Tell him Chrysanthemum is complicating things, and she has to go home."

"I don't—it's too late. Isn't it? I mean, pulling her out of school before a month has gone by—because I can't get a date—doesn't seem too reasonable. How will that look?"

"She's not actually a child!" Noelle all but yells, and Nico holds his hands up in a placating gesture, mumbling more to himself than to her, "I'm well aware."

"This was a stupid fucking idea in the first place! I don't know what he was thinking. I could have spied on you if he wanted to. I mean, I'd give him shitty updates, which is probably why he picked an elf, the greatest elf of all, but honestly! Adding a child into the mix always complicates things. This is ridiculous and it's not even real!"

She's only voicing what he's been thinking all along, but it doesn't make the situation any better. Her passionately agreeing with him only makes him feel worse because there's nothing he can even do at this point. He just has to deal with it from here.

Noelle takes a deep steadying breath and lets it out slowly, "Sorry. I don't mean to snap at you. Lord knows this isn't your fault. But I get so frustrated by dumb shit on the best of days, and with these hormones, god! I have half a mind to call Dad and pick a fight because this is some seriously dumb shit, Tico!"

"I know, Noelle. I know. I'm going—well no, I don't know what I'm going to do. Guess I've got to find someone else. He wants to hang out, be friends and all that, but we kissed on New Year's Eve—"

"Nico!"

"And it was great," Nico barrels on, not letting her distract him from what he's trying to say. "And now all I want to do is kiss him again, but that's all ruined."

Noelle comes around the island and wraps her arms around Nico, hugging him tightly. "My little Tico, this is the saddest I've seen you look in a long time. Maybe you can wait it out? See if he's still interested by the time Chrysanthemum's not in his class?"

"Don't think I can even afford to wait, what, half a year? I've already wasted seven years dicking around while trying to pretend this wasn't all happening no matter what."

Noelle clucks her tongue and steps back, giving him a very pointed stare before her face softens, and she says, "Then you have to talk to Dad and figure something out. Or you've got to tell Elliott she's not your sister and see how he takes it."

A harsh burst of bitterness fills his chest, and he laughs—a sharp and unamused sound in the quiet of the kitchen. "Yeah, already tried. He said, 'I think I'd know if Santa Claus was real,' so here we are. My worst fears confirmed—no one's ever going to believe me, anyway."

Noelle rolls her eyes, but her voice is soft and patient. "Did you say it as a joke, though?"

"No, I mean. He asked me if I was her father, and I said 'Would you believe me if I said she's an elf, and I'm Santa's son?' I was *not* joking."

"Of course, you weren't, but in that situation, he couldn't possibly know you weren't yanking his chain in an effort to uncomplicate things. Though, I guess being Santa's son doesn't exactly uncomplicate things any more than dating your student's brother."

"Well, I can't make him believe me."

Noelle shrugs. "You could show him your powers?"

Nico's cheeks flush, despite his best efforts to tamp down the embarrassment creeping over him, and he splutters, "Displaying is a bit forward even for me."

"It's either that or wait it out. Unless you can figure out how to get Dad to back off, which we both know he's going to double down on his plan since it's gone up in smoke rather than admit he fucked up."

"Those are all terrible options."

"Yeah, but they're what's on the table at this point. Which one sounds the least miserable?"

"Waiting it out sounds the most doable. As you said, I'm very used to closing myself off to happiness, but it's also the one I can't afford to choose. I guess I'll have to call Dad and see what his next brilliant plan is. Can't be any worse than this."

Noelle's eyes widen in shock and her voice is filled to the brim with laughter. "Look at you! I can't believe you'd rather willingly call Dad than Display prematurely. This shows a great amount of growth, Nicholas."

He pushes at her shoulder, playfully and light, "Shut up."

Noelle smirks and Nico does feel marginally better after talking to her, despite how jumbled his head still is. He doesn't want to call Kristoff, and he really doesn't want to waste half a year holding out for someone he's just met if Kristoff doesn't end up conceding he messed things up. For now, he decides the best he can do is go to his room and think.

He knows in his heart the surest way to end this problem is to prove to Elliott he is Santa's son. Showing him—giving him tangible proof he wasn't lying—is unavoidable if they're to have a legitimate future together.

So getting it out the way before it becomes too difficult to bring up wouldn't hurt. He knows telling Elliott now would do nothing but help him. He's fully aware it's the quickest and surest bet, but he can't fathom actually Displaying for Elliot, or anyone, before their first date. It's such an intimate show of trust, or a total disregard of social norms, he can't bring himself to do it. No matter how much he used to posture he didn't care what society deemed appropriate, it's different being the one showing off their powers. Somehow, putting his magic, and thus himself, on display holds far more weight than watching someone else do the same thing.

The first time a guy showed Nico his power before it was considered socially acceptable, Nico thought it was thrilling. He was twenty-four, and Kevin—a bartender a couple years older than him—lit a candle with his finger on their first date. He was so beautiful Nico thought the Display was amazing, no matter how unexpected and unconventional. After Kevin, premature power shows didn't faze Nico in the same way. He realized some people truly didn't care how open they were with their magic.

But now that it's him? Now that he's in a small town like Pine Cove? He honestly can't imagine being able to show Elliott any part of his magic before they've known each other longer. It feels wrong to Display for him as a way to prove something, as a way to get a date. The very idea, combined with everything else he's got on his plate, makes his head spin and his stomach churn uncomfortably. He skips dinner in an attempt to let his nerves settle without having to discuss the issue further, but they only go away as he falls asleep.

In the morning, he wakes to a brief respite of unease. His eyes are bleary, and his mind is foggy with sleep. For a moment, there's nothing to worry him, but then his phone rings, and it's his father. His anxiety comes crashing back down upon him then—everything is falling apart before it's even gotten a chance to start.

"Hello," he groans, not bothering to conceal he's just woken up.

"Good morning, Nicholas. It's been a little over two weeks since you left, and I want to see how you're doing—how things are going."

It's hard to tell over the phone, when he has to rely solely on the inflection of his voice, but Kristoff doesn't sound anything other than genuinely curious, and it makes Nico's heartbeat double. He scrubs a hand over his face and breathes out slowly before saying, "So Chrysanthemum hasn't given you an update, then?"

He can hear the frustrated sigh Kristoff lets out and can imagine the accompanying eye roll as Kristoff grits out, "I didn't send her there to spy on you and send me updates. I sent her there to help you stay on track and answer any questions you may need an immediate response to as she's the most knowledgeable of us all."

Nico huffs out an exasperated breath. "Well, I've got some bad news for you then, Pops. Her being here has done the exact opposite of helping me keep on track."

"What do you mean? Don't be like that Nicholas! She's a good resource, and she's always been so good to you kids. I don't see how her being there can be so bad."

Nico sits up, kicking the blankets off in a fit of frustration, altogether too warm now. "No, you're not understanding. She's quite literally derailed my mission. I actually had a date tonight, but guess what? The guy's her teacher and thinks it's unprofessional to be seeing someone who's related to their student! So yeah, your plan worked out exactly how you wanted."

Kristoff, to Nico's surprise, doesn't respond for quite some time, and when he does, it's a soft, tired sigh, followed by a self-deprecating sort of laugh. "What are the odds? I guess larger in a small town the size of Pine Cove. But I honestly didn't see this being a problem and I'm sorry."

His apology knocks the fight right out of Nico and he has no idea how to respond to it. Twice now, his father has defied Nico's expectations and actually admitted he made a mistake.

"I don't know what to do," he admits in a rare moment of vulnerability he doesn't usually let his father see.

Kristoff takes a sharp breath and Nico can only assume he's pinching the bridge of his nose in thought. A long moment later, Kristoff huffs out, "Let me call you back, Nicholas. I need to talk to your mother."

Kristoff's reaction is shocking. He was expecting his father to justify his decision and tell Nico to move on. Kristoff being so reasonable fills Nico with warm, steady happiness he savors all throughout breakfast. It doesn't even waver as Kristoff calls back.

"I've talked to your mother," he says straight away, sounding resigned. "And while she says we can't bring Chrysanthemum back straight away, we've both agreed it's in your best interest she returns as soon as possible. You've only got so much time left to accomplish your goal, and we can't afford to waste any more. Your mom's thinking the beginning of February."

"What?" His mind's humming with relief, and he can't form a coherent sentence. He's gobsmacked by how easily Kristoff has given up on an idea he came up with.

"We're going to come down there in February and withdraw her from school. Your mom says we should say we've either decided to end our sabbatical much sooner than intended, after realizing it was irresponsible to leave her with you and Noelle for so long, or that your mother missed her too much and I caved on getting her a private tutor to accompany us as we traveled the world."

A loud laugh escapes Nico's mouth, a burst of disbelief he can't contain, and he can barely get his words out around it. "Oh my god, I can't believe this. Is Mom sure she can't read minds? I told Elliott the exact same thing at Chrysanthemum's parent-teacher conference. Told him Chrys wanted a private tutor so she could go with you guys, but you didn't think it was a good idea."

Kristoff laughs, too, and it's a smaller sound than Nico's, but it's joyous to hear. "You and your mother have always shared a similar wavelength. I'm not surprised you both came up with the same concept. Do you think this will work?"

"Yeah, Dad. I think it'll work. I mean, it'll definitely clear up the problem of professionalism. Which just leaves me to charm my way into his heart. Couldn't be easier."

Kristoff's voice is surprisingly gentle when he says, "Nicholas, stop selling yourself short. You are kind and generous and *charming*. This man will be lucky to have you. And if it doesn't work, there are always others. You have time—not much—but you have it. And I do have faith it will all work out."

"Oh, yeah," he says awkwardly, an uncomfortable heat creeping up his neck. He can't remember the last time his father sounded this sure of him. He can't think of a time Kristoff's ever sounded so confident in Nico's abilities instead of doubting his commitment to the family. Nico was not equipped to hear the certainty in Kristoff's voice today. It's too weird, but good and reassuring at the same time. He's waited to hear his father sound like this for so long but forced himself to stop hoping for it. "Thanks, Dad. That means a lot."

"Yeah, of course. I'll let you know once we've got it all squared away and know when we're coming down. But no later than the first week of February for sure. See you then."

He's so content after he hangs up he takes a chance and texts Elliott. "Not a date, but maybe we could still hang out tonight?"

It takes Elliott a full hour to respond and when he reads the response—*I'd love to*—Nico doesn't even care how nervous he was to see what Elliott would say, or how excruciating it was to wait. He's just happy.

Chapter Ten

ELLIOTT AND NICO fall into an easy pattern of friendship after their non-date. They hang out by themselves, or with Eliza, around the coffee shop or around town. Nico doesn't flirt, no matter how much he wants to, but Elliott does. His mannerisms are shy at first; he blushes bright red every time Eliza turns to him with an eyebrow raised in silent question. But Eliza's looks don't seem to deter Elliott, and Nico's grateful, even if he has to forcefully stop himself from preening under Elliott's attention every time he gets it. He doesn't think he succeeds very well, though, because as the days go by, Elliott realizes Nico enjoys the flirting, and increases it tenfold, not even flinching when Eliza levels him with an amused grin and a quirked eyebrow. The flirting, and the confidence Elliott exudes as he does it, makes Nico feel warm and light every time. So even though they're not seeing each other, and there's been no more kissing or talks of dates, Nico thinks they're headed in the right direction. What they're doing—being friends while still interested in each other—is exhilarating.

It's satisfying and keeps the burning anticipation for Chrysanthemum's departure at bay. Mostly. But as January comes to a close and his parents' visit looms near, he can't keep his excitement from Elliott and Eliza anymore. At dinner one night, he lets slip, as casually as he can, the fact his parents are coming to pick Chrysanthemum up and take her around the world with them.

Eliza's eyes widen for a second but then she schools her face, and Nico wouldn't have registered her surprise if it weren't for the way it pushed through the space between them, getting under his skin like an electric shock. However, hers is nothing compared to the onslaught of emotions coming from Elliott. There's confusion, mixed with trepidation, and a gleeful sort of desire flaring up inside Nico via Elliott. The conflict roaring inside him is written all over Elliott's face—it's visible in the purse of his lips and the furrow of his brow—but, when he speaks, his voice is low and even. "What?"

It's not so much a question as an invitation to elaborate, and Nico takes it, keeping his voice as nonchalant as possible. "My mom missed her. I told you she would. Though, I didn't think it would take this long. Anyway, they found a private tutor who was more than willing to uproot their life at such short notice for the opportunity to jet set around the world."

Nico shrugs, and there's not much more he can say, not when Elliott won't believe the actual truth anyway. This little charade is the best they could do in this situation. It was a terrible plan to bring her along from the get-go—he knew that—but Kristoff hadn't. There's no point in dwelling on the past, though; they're making up for Kristoff's bad judgment as best they can, even if the only solution is admittedly abrupt and odd in terms of schooling a supposed ten-year-old.

Nico has to remind himself several times over dinner Chrysanthemum isn't actually ten or even a child. While he tells Elliott and Eliza the plan he has to remember none of this is real, so it doesn't matter how her schooling goes. It doesn't matter at all except...

Elliott purses his lips. Nico's hit with a wave of apprehension, and he laughs, waving his hand in a broad sweeping gesture, like he's picking Elliott's concerns right out of the air, instead of experiencing them grow inside him. "Don't worry. I know what you're thinking, and you don't have to feel bad. This was a ridiculously rash and irresponsible idea of theirs. For as much as my father says he's not as impulsive as me, he doesn't think things through sometimes. But I believe this'll be a better fit. Don't you?"

Nico doesn't look away from Elliott as he waits for a response, but he can see, out of the corner of his eye, the way Eliza's lips quirk at the corners, almost as if she can hear the unspoken *for all of us* left hanging in the air. Within an instant, Elliott's face falls, smooths out, and then erupts into a wide, face-encompassing smile. His smile's always been beautiful, but this one takes Nico's breath away.

"Yeah, I think it will be."

HIS PARENTS COME and Chrysanthemum goes. Elliott later tells Nico Gloria did most of the talking at their meeting—which Nico is eternally grateful for since she's always made better impressions than Kristoff—and how they all agreed this would be a better fit for Chrysanthemum. Yet, her being gone does nothing to change things between Elliott and Nico. They stay in their easy pattern of friendship. They're tipping slowly over into *more*; Nico can feel the shift with every passing day—with every moment he finally flirts back. There's a crackling of electricity surging between them, but neither of them addresses the growing tension, and Nico wonders if the month Chrysanthemum was here was long enough to ruin any chance he had with Elliott. If now the pull of friendship is too important—too good, too easy, too right—to jeopardize by exploring their kiss and rescheduling their canceled date.

He doesn't realize what the problem may be until he's at work with Addison and she asks him if he and Elliott are doing anything for Valentine's Day.

Nico's mouth turns down in an exaggerated frown as he responds, playfully chiding, "You're very nosy."

Addison laughs, a bubbling sound that floats through the air and makes Nico laugh too. "Yes, I do know." She shrugs like it's nothing, and it isn't, not when he's known nosier adults. Hell, Noelle's one of the nosiest people he's ever met and he's known her all his life—he's used to prying at this point. So when Addison raises her eyebrow and tilts her head to the side, questioning, he answers truthfully. "We're not actually a thing, you know."

Addison's nostrils flare and her exasperated sigh mixes with the flutter of annoyance building in Nico's stomach to let him know she doesn't believe him in the slightest.

"We're not! I think I'd know."

There's mutual attraction between the two—their interest growing stronger as the days pass—but Nico would know if they crossed the line into something more *established.* He would.

No matter how much he wants them to have rescheduled their canceled date by now, they haven't. They're still hanging in limbo, tiptoeing around each other's interest while shamelessly flirting.

The conversation is dropped as a new rush of customers comes in, but as the orders dwindle, the opportunity arises for Addison to continue the conversation as if it never stopped. "I see you two interact. Maybe you're not *a thing,* but you've definitely got *a* thing, you know? It's obvious. Painfully so, actually."

She leans against the counter, crossing her arms expectantly, and Nico nods—there's no denying her assessment.

"Maybe Valentine's Day is what's holding you back?"

Nico considers it, but he didn't even remember it was coming until right now. The truth is he's waiting for Elliott to make the first move because some habits die hard. "Nah, I don't think that's what it is."

"Maybe not for you, but it could be for him. In my experience boys are weird as shit when it comes to this holiday. Girls on the other hand..."

Again, he thinks she's right. "You're very observant."

"We can't all be as oblivious as you," she says with a smirk.

"I guess we'll have to wait out the holiday then."

"Oh my god," Addison says as she buries her face in her hands. She pulls her hands away and laughs at Nico. "As I said, boys and their hang-ups about the holiday."

"I don't have any hang-ups!"

She pushes off the counter and pokes him in the chest. "Then ask him out! It doesn't have to be for Valentine's Day, but waiting until *after* the day to even broach the subject, when you both obviously have a thing for each other, is dumb as hell."

He watches the door as she settles behind the cash register and shakes his head—in the short time they've known each other, Nico has grown quite fond of the way she always speaks her mind. "Your bluntness never ceases to amaze me, Addison."

She sounds like he's given her the best compliment in the world when she says, "It's one of my finer qualities."

Nico snorts, and then, just like that, the conversation is over. He's left wondering if he's brave enough to make the first move, or if it's worth riding it out and waiting to see where Elliott goes from here. Someone has to cave eventually, right? Elliott will definitely make a move. It doesn't have to be Nico to put himself out there. He can wait. He's waited this long, what's a bit more?

In the end, Elliott says nothing, and Nico's patience wars with his desire to not be the one making the first move. They continue flirting and tiptoeing around the obvious attraction they both have all while ignoring the possibility of another date. Everything stays as it has been since they left Winnie's on New Year's Eve. Neither of them disturbs the status quo of friendship, and Nico comes to the conclusion he's going to have to be the one to make a move if he ever wants to reach uncharted territory with Elliott.

Chapter Eleven

NICO INTENDED TO spend Valentine's Day holed up in his room avoiding the low achy longing building in his chest over this game he and Elliott are playing with each other. Instead, he ends up at the coffee shop despite not being scheduled for the day. Noelle is hosting an event and she's extended the hours of the shop. It's supposed to be for singles only, but mostly, Nico thinks, people are here for the half-price, heart-shaped cookies and the teeth-rotting, sweet pink coffee concoction she's made especially for the day.

She roped him into taking photos, saying it'd be nice to frame some of his work for the shop and update her website, but he knows she's hoping to spark his interest in doing photography again. He hasn't even touched his camera since Christmas, and he hasn't taken any photos outside of work since three gigs ago. He's wanted to, but life got in the way. Then he lost the desire. And *now?* Well now, it feels like too much to start again. But Noelle gave him her patented "please, Nic, for me?" pout and he caved as quickly as ever. For as stubborn as he could be, he always crumbled for her.

So here he is, taking pictures of the people in Kahveci's, finally enjoying himself enough to stop fretting over the tension building between him and Elliott and how he has no idea what to do about it—or how to make the first move.

Or at least, he was distracted until the moment he sees Elliott come down from his apartment upstairs. He's heading straight for Nico, directing one of his broad, face-encompassing smiles at him, and Nico's breath hitches in his throat. His chest aches with the beauty of it, stomach fluttering under the attention. He didn't plan on seeing Elliot tonight, but now that he has, well, he's glad Noelle dragged him out for this. He not sure how to propel them forward out of this stalemate but any excuse to hang out with Elliott is always good by him.

"Fancy seeing you here," Elliott says as he sidles up next to Nico, knocking their hips together. The touch sends an actual shock through him, and Elliott laughs, then says, "You and your static electricity."

This happens a lot between them now, and Nico's starting to think it, along with the start-and-stop snowing from when he first arrived, has something to do with his powers. He needs to broach the subject with his dad; it's getting out of hand.

"Yeah," Nico says, a beat too late, but Elliott doesn't seem to mind. His eyes are sweeping through the coffee shop, taking in all the people. Then they settle on the camera in Nico's hands, and his eyebrows knit together for a moment before he asks, "You're into photography?"

"Eh, used to be," he shrugs. "I mean, no. I *am* into photography, but I've kind of lost my drive for it. Been a while since I've taken pictures of anything I love to photograph, y'know? If I'm honest. I do a lot of destination weddings so I can travel, but weddings weren't on my radar when I decided to go to school for photography."

Elliott hums, considering Nico's words, and then his mouth twists into a smile, teasing. "Traveling around the world and photographing people on one of the happiest days of their lives does sound like a real drag."

Nico elbows Elliott, laughing. "Oh shut up. That's not what I meant."

"What did you dream of doing, then?"

"Don't laugh at me, but," he says, checking to make sure Elliott nods before continuing, "I wanted to be a concert photographer. God, the ideal for me back then was to travel with a band and be their personal photographer, but that never panned out."

"I'm starting to think you enjoy traveling."

"Yeah, I do. New people, new places, new foods. What's not to love?"

"Planes." Elliott's lips fan out in a thin line, grimacing.

"You don't like to fly?"

"Well, I've never actually been on a plane, but the idea of it makes me nervous, so..."

Nico can't hold back his surprise. "Oh my god, seriously?"

Elliott ducks his head, embarrassed, and Nico's stomach drops—he didn't mean to make him feel bad. "Never been outside of Pine Cove very much, actually."

"Oh man, we're going to have to fix that," Nico soothes. "You'll have to come to New York with me or something. I've still got an apartment there. We could go for a weekend."

He says it before he realizes how presumptuous it may sound—they haven't even discussed another date yet!—and Nico's cheeks start to burn. But Elliott smiles, soft and a little shy and Nico breathes easier. Elliott's voice is hushed and scratchy, like he's talking around a lump in his throat, and Nico's mouth dries out as Elliott says, "Yeah, I'd like that."

"Well in that case—" Nico says, swallowing down his nerves, emboldened by Elliott's obvious interest. "—I think it's time we rescheduled our date."

It's Elliott's turn to blush, mouth twitching in a smile as the pink expands over his nose and across his cheeks. It's adorable. He ducks his head again, studying his shoes as he scratches at the back of his neck, and says, "Yeah. Yeah. I think it is."

Nico's stomach swoops, heart hammering, head spinning with relief. He'd wanted Elliott to make the move, and for a while, he was sure he would be the one to broach the subject—he'd been the one to initiate their kiss on New Year's Eve and set up their initial date, after all. It had become clear over the last few weeks, though, that Elliott shifted between confidence and shyness in the blink of an eye. The moment Nico started flirting back Elliott started stumbling over his responses, cheeks burning bright red at the attention. It felt satisfying, getting that response from him, but it also made Nico feel less ridiculous for how bumbling and awkward he'd been this entire time. It felt nice to be on the same page as someone else, to not be the only one nervous as hell all the time.

"Well, good," Nico says, a touch too loud, even over the noise of the coffee shop. "Good. I'm glad," Nico says, quieter, surer this time.

His bubbling nerves and excitement mix with the nervous energy Elliott's emitting, and now Nico wants to go for a run, needs to move before these feelings take him over. He hadn't actually thought of a place to go since this was an impulsive decision. He can't think straight and starts rambling. "Should we go back to the same place for our date? Or is it bad luck? I think it might be bad luck. Don't want to start off on the wrong foot. We should go somewhere different. Yeah. Definitely different place. Has to be a jinx to go to the same place you had to cancel with."

Elliott's laughing next to him, shoulders shaking with the force of it, and Nico's blushing again. His rambling seems to have allowed Elliott to regain some of his confidence, enough to say, voice still light with laughter, "I don't think it'll be a jinx if we go to Maxine's, but if you do, then I think we shouldn't. We could go—"

"Nico!" Noelle shouts, running up to him and cutting Elliott off midsentence. Her eyes are wide, and he can feel disbelief crawling under his skin. "What are you still doing here?"

Nico blinks, holding up his camera, feeling dumbfounded. "You asked me to be here? You told me to take pictures!"

She gives him a sharp look and the disbelief grows into annoyance. He can feel it clawing at his skin, and he wants to roll his eyes, tell her to back off, but he doesn't. He stays quiet and lets her respond, "I don't need you anymore. I'm sure you got enough pictures you can show them to me later. Thanks for doing this for me."

Her voice is brusque and demanding. She puts her hand on his side and pushes. "Come on, out, out, out. Go, go, go."

He stumbles into Elliott with the force of her motion. Elliot laughs, his hand coming up to brace Nico's side, steadying him. He's now fully leaning into Elliott's space— their sides pressed together—and Noelle's giving Nico a smug, self-satisfied smirk. Nico rolls his eyes. She's pushing them together, literally, because she's more impatient than anyone he's ever met.

He curls his arm around Elliott, lets his hand fall to the small of his back, and nudges him forward. "I see we're no longer welcome in my very own place of work. Come on."

Elliott's practically humming with happiness as they walk out of Kahveci's, and same as ever, his good mood is infectious. The feeling thrums through Nico's fingertips, where he's touching Elliott, and travels up his arm before settling warm in his chest.

They're walking down the street, Nico trying to figure out where they should go other than Maxine's, when Elliott stops and says, "There's a gallery opening in Portland this Saturday, and I was planning on going."

His cheeks are red, and Nico thinks it's not only the cold causing it. Elliott ducks his head and continues, mumbling at first, voice growing more confident as he goes. "There's a painting there I wanted to check out—it's of my favorite pop star. The drive's a bit long, and I don't know if you'd want to, but you like photography and there's that there, too, and there're way more options down there than there are here. And I was thinking, if you want, of course, you could join me? Since Maxine's is out of the picture now."

"Oh, I'd love that, actually."

"Okay, yeah, yeah. Let's do that then. Saturday. We can make a day of it."

SATURDAY IS GOOD until the moment they leave the gallery and run into Taylor holding hands with another guy steps outside the building.

Elliott's tipsy from too much champagne, and Nico's reveling in the way Elliott wraps his arm around his shoulders as they walk, warmth blooming in his chest and snaking out through his veins as they go. There was a painting at the gallery Elliott loved. So much so, he spent fifteen minutes telling Nico all about the subject—a pop star who Nico was vaguely familiar with, A. B. Cerise. He's one of Elliott's and Eliza's favorites—the one Elliott mentioned when he invited him out for this—and by the way his eyes lit up and his cheeks flushed the more he talked, Nico could tell he was quite a big fan. Seeing him talk so passionately was endearing and Nico easily got lost in the light airy burst of enthusiasm sweeping over him because of Elliott.

Elliott is bemoaning the lack of dates for A. B.'s summer tour anywhere near Pine Cove when Nico registers a prick of curiosity under the heavy spike of Elliott's annoyance. Nico hears his name and his attention is drawn away from a babbling Elliot.

"Nico, is that you?" the voice repeats, and there's the prickling sensation of curiosity again.

He stops short, gawking at the familiar face, and Elliott's fingers tighten against his shoulder as he moves to stop with Nico.

"Taylor." He says, lost for words. *How is this happening? Is the world fucking with me?*

Taylor's voice is strong and curious, carrying in a way that makes Nico snap out of his own thoughts. "What are you doing here? Aren't you in New York?"

Elliott's fingers twitch against his shoulder, and Nico senses his apprehension and nerves bubbling inside him—they're too big, almost to the point of bursting already. Nico doesn't want Elliott to move his arm.

"I am. Or I was. But um." God, he hates how tongue-tied Taylor makes him. "Yeah, I'm in Pine Cove for the time being. Helping Noelle out for the year. Elliott brought me out for the gallery opening. Do you live here noow?"

Taylor's focus darts to Elliott's face and then to where his hand is hanging over Nico's shoulder, and he tenses by Nico's side. Nico can do nothing to stop the way Elliott's bubbling nerves burst inside him, replaced in an instant with a fizzling disappointment as Elliott pulls away from Nico. Elliott's hand hangs limply at his side, but his knuckles brush against Nico's, and the touch calms his own nerves momentarily.

Taylor starts to laugh, and Elliott twines his fingers through Nico's, a surge of protective heat coursing up Nico's spine as they touch. "God, Nico. You always did have a shit memory. I'm from here."

"Oh, Jesus," Nico says, cheeks burning. "In my defense, it has been a long time since we spoke. Not considering the last time."

Taylor's date raises an eyebrow, and Nico finally takes a moment to give him a once-over, registering his appearance. He's handsome with swooping black hair and the makings of a beard that works for him despite its lack of fullness. His dark brown eyes bore into Nico, sizing him up for a moment before an understanding washes over his face. "Oh, this is *the Nico*."

"The Nico? I'm assuming there's a story here." Elliott's voice is tight, and his hand twitches in Nico's as Nico's stomach curls uncomfortably. This is not the end he had in mind for their date.

"Yeah, hon, this is Nico." There's laughter in Taylor's voice, and he looks at his date with a soft, gentle affection all too familiar to Nico. Instead of being jealous or wanting it to be turned on him as it once was, Nico is relieved. He's happy Taylor found someone else, but above all, he's glad to recognize the relief growing inside him as he watches Taylor interact with this man. He's only started to get to know Elliott, but he loves where they're headed, and he's pleased life led him this way. For the first time, Nico is content with his decision to let Taylor go— It allowed him to find Elliott, after all.

Taylor's date reaches forward to shake Nico's hand, introducing himself. "Well Nico, it's nice to meet you. I'm Daniel."

There's a beat of silence as he settles back in against Taylor's side and then he smiles. Nico's hit with a wave of pure, unadulterated joy, and he knows the source before the words are even coming out of Daniel's mouth. "I guess I owe you some thanks for breaking his heart—"

"Danny!" Taylor says at the same time Elliott draws in a sharp breath, but Daniel keeps going: his joy almost entirely overshadowing the surge of embarrassment coming from Taylor.

"Because we just got engaged, and I've never been happier. So. Yeah."

It's the most awkward engagement announcement Nico's ever been a part of. But Daniel's words make Elliott's nerves peter out, and Nico thinks it's safe to say he's caught on to Taylor not being a threat or obstacle to their budding relationship. That's a relief. A big relief. The last thing he needed was another bump in the road to happiness with Elliott—they'd already waited so long for this date he couldn't imagine mustering up the patience to wait for another if this night turned sour because of this run-in.

"Oh, Taylor. Congratulations! I'm so happy for you, man."

To his complete shock, the words were easy to say, not even a little bit of a lie. He is happy for him. He's happy Taylor's taken, happy he's no longer in Nico's life, and happy he had this weird run-in to confirm for himself he didn't mess up his entire love life by letting Taylor go. He's delighted life moved on despite their heartache and they could both find joy outside each other.

Throughout the last few years, Nico's anxiety surrounding his inability to find love only grew; he truly believed he lost his chance at happiness when he walked away from Taylor. Now with Elliott, though, he realizes he was only convincing himself he lost his chance as a form of punishment—as if he didn't deserve to want love anymore. There's a new and exciting bond blooming between him and Elliott, and he's relieved he finally let himself have this. It's exhilarating to allow himself the freedom to want, and know he deserves, to love again.

"So," Elliott says as they leave Taylor and Daniel behind. His hand is back around Nico's shoulder, fingers curling into the fabric of his shirt, as they approach Nico's car. "You're a real big heartbreaker?"

His voice is light and teasing, and the feeling building inside Nico matches Elliott's tone. A laugh escapes Nico, it's loud in the quiet parking garage, but he can't help it—he's so overjoyed Elliott didn't get turned off by this run-in. "Yeah, that's me. Breaking hearts since twenty-two."

Elliott's hand moves from his shoulder. Nico swallows down disappointment at the loss of contact only for Elliott's hand to find its way to the back of Nico's neck, gently guiding him around so they're facing each other. Elliott laughs low and breathy and leans forward, whispering, "I do hope to be the end to this devastating little habit of yours."

Nico's laugh is lost as Elliott closes the small gap between their mouths, and it's safe to say this has been one of his best first dates ever.

Chapter Twelve

THEIR SECOND DATE is the Friday after their first and they're meant to be having a movie night at Nico's apartment. Elliott was absolutely insulted three days before when he found out Nico had never seen an *Iron Man* movie and insisted they remedy such an offense as soon as possible. Instead, a kiss on the couch as they settle in to start the movie turns into Elliott scrambling onto Nico's lap, grinding his hips against Nico until it's too much and not enough at all. He slips a hand between them, palming Nico through the fabric of his jeans, and then laughs into his shoulder at the low, throaty groan Nico lets out at the touch. They don't go to Nico's bedroom. They don't take a moment to shuck their clothes off or give themselves more space. Both are too impatient, too desperate for relief to do anything but hurriedly undo zippers and make just enough room to get their hands around each other. It's clumsy and a little rough, but after, when Elliott drops his head on Nico's shoulder and sighs, hot against the crook of his neck, it's perfect.

It's messy though—*they're* a mess—and Nico can only sit there with Elliott slumped against him, breathing against his skin, for so long before the need to be *clean* overwhelms him. Nico untangles himself from Elliott, rolling him off of his lap and onto the couch and heads to his room under the pretense of finding Elliott something clean to wear.

He stops at the hallway and turns back to Elliott. He's still sitting on the couch—his cheeks are flushed bright pink, his hair mussed—and Nico wants him back in touching distance. He tries to keep the desire from clouding his voice, tries to keep his voice steady and even, because he doesn't want to come across as needy as he says, "Are you going to stay there?"

"Mm, thinking about it," Elliott says.

"You can't just sit on my couch with come all over your clothes. What sort of host would I be if I let you do that?"

"A terrible one if I'm honest," Elliott laughs. His eyes are twinkling as he pushes himself off the couch to join Nico.

"Exactly," Nico exhales, pleased to have Elliott in his space again, breath catching in his throat as Elliott presses in behind him.

"You're very considerate," he says against the shell of Nico's ear, and then Nico's eagerly turning around, leaning up and in to kiss Elliott. Nico revels in the soft, pleased sound Elliott makes at the back of his throat when he does and lets himself unabashedly want without embarrassment.

The urge for a change of clothes is replaced by the need for no clothes at all the moment Elliott deepens the kiss. They're both scrambling to get each other's shirts off, stumbling over each other as Nico tries to lead them backward to his room, to his bed. Once there...once Nico's legs hit the edge of the mattress, it's easy for them to detangle from each other long enough to get their clothes off. Then they're back on each other, Elliott pushing Nico onto the mattress, kissing down his jaw, over the column of his throat, stopping at his collarbone to drag his teeth against the soft skin. He moves slowly, taking his time working his mouth down over Nico's skin, pausing to glance at Nico every time he lets out a sound, cataloging them, storing them away for future reference. The slow, steady pace of Elliott's mouth trailing down his body is almost too much. Elliott's mouth is hovering right above the head of his cock, breath warm and damp over the sensitive skin, making Nico desperate and needy.

The sound he makes when Elliott finally takes him between his lips is somewhere between a gasp and a laugh because he didn't expect someone who blushes so deeply while receiving a compliment to be this good at giving head, to be so sure of every move he makes. He fists the sheets and resists the urge to buck up into his mouth, leaving Nico hoping Elliott never stops surprising him. He's vaguely aware of how vocal he's being, how embarrassed he'd normally be by the sounds coming out of his mouth, but it's so good he doesn't care. Nico believes Elliott deserves to hear how easily he's taking him apart, how much he's making him feel.

He comes so hard he sees spots, all sounds dying out in the wake of his orgasm, and the only thing left to hear is his ragged, erratic breathing. Elliott wipes his mouth against the back of his hand and sits back against his heels, grinning smugly at Nico, "Did you enjoy yourself?"

"Shut up," he says, surging forward to kiss Elliott, pulling him down and flipping them over so Elliott's lying against the bed now.

He matches Elliott's pace from before, then slows it down even further, teasing Elliott until he's begging, soft and breathy, "Nico, please."

He pulls away, letting his hands ghost over Elliott's skin. He waits, watching as Elliott shivers beneath Nico's not-quite-there touch. He holds out for one, two, three, pounding heartbeats before he crumbles against Elliott's pleas and swallows him down.

Afterward, they lie there for a long moment, silent save for their heavy breathing until Elliott laughs. "You know, *Iron Man* wasn't a plot to get you in bed. But..."

Nico laughs, too, and turns into Elliott's side. "No, I'm sure you would've saved that for at least *Iron Man 2*."

THEY ATTEMPT TO watch *Iron Man* another five times, to no avail, before Elliott gives up and insists on inviting Eliza to join them for movie night in an effort to force Nico to pay attention. It doesn't work out as well as Elliott wanted. Eliza spends the entire movie talking, but they do make it all the way to the end without putting their hands on each other, so Nico counts it as a win. Or really, a loss by his standards, but Elliott is happy Nico's at least seen the whole movie, so Nico thinks of it as a success. As February dwindles to a close and March speeds right on by, Nico learns making Elliott happy is one of life's greatest pleasures, at least for him.

That's why, even though he has the opening shift in the morning, he's sitting here on Elliott's couch on a Thursday night as midnight creeps by with Elliott's head in his lap, running his fingers through his sweat-damp curls, in an attempt to soothe him to sleep.

"Seems your fever finally broke," he mumbles, and Elliott's eyes flutter open, glassy and distant. "You look like shit, babe. Let's get you to bed."

"No," Elliott whines. "Don't want to move. Feel terrible."

"You can't be comfortable like this," Nico huffs out in disbelief. "You'll have more room to stretch your legs out in bed. Come on, I'll even lay with you."

"Hmmm," Elliott considers. His eyes are still glistening, but this time there's a softer, more familiar quality to them.

It fills him with a deep, radiating warmth, and Nico sighs, letting Elliott have his way for a moment longer. "Fine, but in five minutes, I'm taking you to bed whether you want or not! And I'd really prefer not to carry you. I have terrible upper-body strength, and you're so tall. Do you want me to embarrass myself?"

Elliott laughs until it turns into a cough and then Nico's pushing at his shoulders and helping him up. "Okay, okay. I'm putting my foot down now. We're going to bed. Come on."

Elliott whimpers as they get up, and Nico wraps his arm around his waist, steadying him as he trips over Nico's feet.

"Easy there. You're clumsy on the best of days, don't move so fast."

Once in bed, Elliott lies on his side and waits for Nico to join him under the duvet, and then sighs heavily against the thin fabric of Nico's shirt as he settles his head on Nico's chest.

"Thank you," Elliott says through a yawn, cuddling up closer to him. Nico's likely to fall asleep here, with Elliott's long limbs curled around him. "You're the best boyfriend I've ever had."

Nico's body tenses for a brief moment—they'd never labeled themselves before—but then he relaxes, wraps his arms around Nico, and hugs him tight. A familiar, comforting hum of happiness radiates from Elliott, dancing along and through Nico's skin to settle warmly in his chest, and Nico understands this isn't Elliott babbling through a fever haze. Nico knows the feeling seeping into his heart intimately. It's something he experiences every time he's with Elliott, something that thrums through him with the intensity of a wave breaking. It's so familiar he even recognizes he experiences it outside of Elliott's emotions. He feels it when Elliott's not even around, when he's only thinking of him, or telling Noelle something he's said. It's warm and lovely and fills his stomach with butterflies while making his heart flutter any time Elliott's name is mentioned.

It's late, and he's exhausted, and 'love' flashes through his mind as he presses a kiss to Elliott's head. A cold, clamminess settles in his stomach at first, but then he closes his eyes and focuses on Elliott in his arms. His breathing is slowing and he's starting to relax against Nico's chest, and Nico realizes love isn't too far from being true. There's nowhere else he'd rather be than right here with Elliott.

He leans down and presses a kiss against Elliott's hair, smiling as he lets out a soft, pleased little sigh. "Yeah, you're a pretty great boyfriend yourself. I'll even consider forgiving you if I end up getting sick from all this cuddling."

Elliott doesn't respond, his breathing slow and even, and Nico knows, without checking, all from the calm sensation washing over him, Elliott's finally fallen asleep.

NICO LEAVES WATER, a dose of cold medicine, and a note on Elliott's nightstand when he heads to work in the morning. He only gets a few hours of sleep, and his shift is as miserable as he expected it to be, when he woke up this morning, but it's all worth it when he goes back up to Elliott's apartment and is greeted at the door by a beaming Elliott.

"Good afternoon, sunshine!"

"You look better," Nico says, leaning up to catch Elliott's mouth in a quick kiss.

"Ugh, you're going to get sick if you keep doing that," he says, pulling away with a crinkled nose and a pout.

"Mmm. I think all the breathing on me you've done since Wednesday would do me in anyway. If I get sick, which I very rarely do, I get sick. It's not a big deal. But it will be your turn to take care of me."

"I guess I can deal with that," Elliott sighs.

"You're a good man, Elliott Laska," Nico teases, basking in the sound of Elliott's laugh and the brightness of his eyes, which has nothing to do with his fever from yesterday. He makes his way to Elliott's bedroom, calling back as he goes, "Now come on, I'm falling asleep as we speak! I need a nap."

"I just woke up!" Elliott calls back and Nico frowns.

He's glad he's turned away from Elliott and can hide his disappointment, glad his voice comes out teasing instead of petulant, "Whose fault is it I got so little sleep? Definitely not my fault!"

Elliott's standing behind him now, guiding him toward the bed with a steady hand on his back. "You make a fair point. You sleep. I've got some stuff to catch up with anyway. It'll make me feel less terrible for calling out this morning if I at least do some work."

Nico's now lying in Elliott's bed, duvet pulled up to his chin, eyelids heavy with exhaustion. He yawns, nearly losing his battle against staving off sleep, but he has something to say before he gives in, wanting to soothe Elliott's nerves before he passes out. "Don't fret over calling out. You had a fever! Aren't there rules about that? You would've gotten all the kiddos sick and then felt even worse. Besides, now look at you! Almost all better. I can't even tell you were snot riddled and feverish yesterday. You only seem a little tired now. Taking the day off did that for you."

Elliott runs his fingers through Nico's hair, huffing out a breath of laughter. "Yeah, you're right."

His fingers stall in Nico's hair for a moment, and he mumbles something Nico doesn't understand, but the sound of his voice makes Nico feel warm and safe and then he's sleeping, dreaming of the Northern Realm. It's not on fire this time, everything mostly the way he left it. The Great Flake is a little wilted, not nearly as beautiful as it is in real life, but there's no fire, and when Nico wakes later to the smell of cookies, he thinks his dream must mean something good. It's not perfect, and he's not quite in love, but he's headed there; the seeds are being planted and biding their time until they're ready to bloom. He's confident in his feelings and sure the dwindling intensity of his nightmare detailing the destruction of the Northern Realm is a reflection of his own shrinking anxiety.

He's calm and rejuvenated as he leaves Elliott's room and joins him in the kitchen right as he's placing cookies on a cooling rack. Elliott glances up and smiles. "Your hair is a mess."

Nico runs a hand through his hair and stifles a yawn. "Mm. Usually is when I wake up."

Elliott's gaze darts over Nico's hair, searching for something, his brow furrowing in confusion. He sets the spatula down, cookies left forgotten, as he walks forward to stand in front of Nico. He runs his fingers through the front part of Nico's hair, just as he did when Nico was falling asleep. "Huh. I could have sworn I saw some gray in your hair earlier. Now it's as black as ever."

Nico's hand instinctively goes to his hair, heartbeat ticking up—this can't be happening already. It's too soon and there's absolutely no way. He's only just accepted the feeling was planted; he's not ready for it to physically manifest. Not yet.

Elliott misinterprets his shock and giggles, "Don't worry. I think a little salt and pepper will suit you."

Nico can't muster anything more than a hum of agreement, his mind reeling at the idea of his hair already silvering, when nothing similar happened once in his entire time with Taylor—and they were together for years.

"Well that's good," he manages to say after Elliott returns to his cookies. "I'm destined for it. Not a single man in my family has avoided it."

"I think it'll suit you," Elliott says with such certainty it makes Nico's heart skip a beat. It almost lessens his nervous dread about completing the Santafication process. Almost, but not quite. He wonders if falling in love will ever put a stop to all his negative emotions surrounding this holiday and his duties to his family and the world. He wonders if he's destined to be unhappy with his life's work, no matter if he's in love or not.

"Nico, are you still with me?"

Nico blinks and there's Elliott in front of him again. This time he's holding out a cookie for Nico in one hand while he rests the other on Nico's face, brushing his thumb across his cheekbone. The touch is gentle and grounding and Nico shakes his head, clearing the remnants of sleep and the jitters he gets every time he imagines becoming Santa. "Yeah, sorry. Just thinking. What kind of cookies did you make?"

"Iced oatmeal. My mom used to make them for me when I was sick."

Nico takes the proffered cookie and says, "Don't take it personally if I don't like it, okay? I'm not much of a cookie guy."

Elliott's eyes narrow in disbelief. "First, this is the best cookie ever. Even when my mom doesn't make it. Second, everyone loves cookies."

Nico shrugs. "I don't know. I never really have."

A wave of disbelief hits Nico with such strength, he laughs. He's never been the best liar—no point when he can't get away with it—but he thinks he's going to have to pretend to appreciate this cookie to placate Elliot. He takes a bite and is surprised he actually does enjoy it.

The smug smile Elliott gives him when he takes another bite is beautiful, and if Elliott wasn't recovering from a cold and so opposed to the idea, Nico would wipe the smirk off his face with a kiss. Instead, he refrains and says, "Who knew all it took for me to love a cookie is for my boyfriend to make them for me?"

"Boyfriend?" Elliott asks and Nico nearly drops his cookie from the force with which Elliott's surprise hits him square in the chest.

"Yeah...uh...well," Nico stutters. There's something under Elliott's surprise, though, a humming sensation deep in the pit of his stomach letting Nico know he's not upset, and this is the familiar, happiness he pinpointed last night, building in strength. "You called me that last night. I mean, you were falling asleep, but I figured..."

He trails off, not knowing what else to say, but the affection in his stomach is only growing and Elliott's smile is transforming his face into something soft and angelic and Nico's heart beats a tad quicker as Elliott says, "Yeah, boyfriend. I like that."

Nico can't resist the urge to kiss him this time, but Elliott doesn't seem to mind. He leans into Nico's lips and deepens the kiss on his own, and Nico thinks the silvering makes sense—this is starting to feel a lot like love.

Chapter Thirteen

KRISTOFF CALLS TO check up on Nico's progress the morning he's meant to leave for his long weekend away with Elliott, Eliza, and her sometimes partner, Rayna. Every talk with his father has gone better than the last, especially since Valentine's Day, when he and Elliott had finally given it another go, but it still puts Nico on edge hearing from him. Nico doesn't think such reactionary annoyance will ever fully fade.

"Nicholas," he says by way of greeting. "How are things with you and Elliott going?"

"They're good. They're great," he says and then, before he can convince himself not to, he adds, "There's actually something I needed to ask you, but you have got to promise not to make a big deal out of it."

Kristoff takes a deep breath and lets it out just as slowly. "I can't make any guarantees."

His honesty startles a laugh out of Nico, and now that he's mentioned it, there's no way he can get out of asking. He does want to know, though, so he pushes forward, hoping his father can at least mitigate his reaction until Nico's hung up.

"Okay. Fine. At least you're being upfront. Anyway, this thing's been happening. So look, I know when I've fallen in love my hair's going to turn silver and all that. But lately, Elliott's been noticing random spots of silver, or what he thinks is gray, in my hair, but by the time I get to a mirror, it's gone. What's that about?"

"Oh, Nicholas! Things aren't just going well, then. They're going fantastic!"

Kristoff's voice is brimming with excitement, and this is what Nico was afraid of—he didn't want him to take this as too much of a good sign.

"So I assume I'm on the right track, then," he says, trying to keep the growing frustration out of his voice. His father's just happy he's finally making progress; he knows that.

"Yes. Random localized silvering of the hair generally begins when you truly start feeling committed to someone. It's brought on when you have a particularly strong surge of emotion. It's like how earlier you were making it randomly snow and shocking Elliott every time you touched. The shocks, more than the snow, are connected to your feelings for the person. It'll happen when you're feeling something particularly intense. Whereas, the snow, from what I gathered from the reading I did into past Santa's journals—because that never happened to me—is something to do with your powers going berserk due to your own, mostly tumultuous, emotions."

"So what you're saying is I'm falling in love."

There's a lump forming in his throat and his father's voice, unmistakably proud, only makes it grow. "Yes, son. It does appear so."

"Okay," Nico sighs.

"You don't sound pleased."

"I-uh. Listen, I'm happy right now, and I can hear how happy you are this is happening, but I don't want you getting your hopes up. I don't want to get my hopes up when there's no way of knowing at this point it'll be enough. There's no way of knowing yet if I'll finish the Santafication in time."

Kristoff takes another long, drawn-out breath and lets it out with a tired sigh. "You have to have faith in the process, Nico."

Nico's so taken aback by his father calling him by his nickname for the first time in forever—actually, Nico can't remember a time he's been called anything but Nicholas by his dad—he doesn't have time to level him with any snark before Kristoff continues.

"I know, in large part, this has to do with the pressure I have put on you to fall in love. I know that. But, please, don't let my constant reminders get in the way of your happiness. I know it's not ideal for this family and our business to be tied up so deeply with our relationships, but these are the cards we've been dealt for generations now. And, of course, you can feel whatever way you want, but this is what being a Hamurişi man entails. You've found someone who's igniting the process, who's making you feel the things you're expected to feel. Don't let your expectations take the good out of what you're experiencing. Of course, it's good not to get your hopes up, but don't guard your heart so tightly you sabotage what you have. Doing so would hurt you the most. Not our family."

"Okay, yeah. Okay. You're right," Nico admits, and Kristoff chuckles.

"I know how hard that must be for you to say, Nicholas."

"Terribly so," he laughs. The mood is light and almost teasing and it's nice. He's not had this level of friendliness with his father in a long time. It's good and what he's said, no matter how hard it will be for him to internalize, does make sense. Noelle and Chrysanthemum said the same months ago: he can't let his expectations get in the way of his happiness. He has to take care of his heart first and hope everything else falls in place after. And for once, he ends a phone call with his father without his skin crawling. He feels good and ready for the weekend with his friends and Elliott.

RAYNA, WHO IS tall and slender, with dark skin that shimmers in the sun, is the life of the weekend. They talk nonstop, hands moving a mile a minute as they gesticulate, and they're the first person Nico's ever witnessed keeping Eliza on her toes. The two of them stay out late and wake up early and allow Elliott and Nico absolutely no input on what they do during the day. They duck their heads together and giggle over a shared joke whenever Nico even thinks to complain, and before Nico has a chance to consider if it's him they're laughing at, Elliott assures him this is how they've always been, and it's nice to finally have someone here to share in being bossed around.

On the last night of their little vacation, Eliza and Rayna leave Elliott and Nico in the hotel room with the promise to return in no less than two hours with a surprise. Elliott shares a look with Eliza as they leave, and the moment the door shuts, Elliott is crowding into Nico's space, kissing him like he's been waiting this whole time to get his mouth on Nico's. He wastes no time in getting his hands under Nico's clothes, undressing him with sure, steady hands. Nico sighs against Elliott's mouth at the way he takes control—this is always his favorite part.

Afterward, when Nico's chest is heaving and he's trying to catch his breath, Elliott props up on one elbow and smirks down at Nico, "Your postcoital flush is a sight for sore eyes."

His laughing response is all-encompassing—Nico's body shakes with it, and he turns into Elliott's side, trying to catch his breath. Elliott wraps his arm around Nico's side, fingers brushing against his spine, making him shiver.

"Please, babe," Nico says, gasping for air. "Don't say things like postcoital."

"Fine, if you insist. Postfornication doesn't have the same ring to it, though."

Nico pushes at Elliott's chest, groaning, "You're the worst, and I don't even know why I like you."

Elliott quirks an eyebrow. "Is that so?"

"Yes, it is," he says, trying to sound serious and failing when Elliott puts a hand to his chest and pouts. "Nico, your words hurt."

"Shh. You love it."

Elliott nods, carding his fingers through the hair at the nape of Nico's neck; his nails gently scrape Nico's skin, and Nico's eyes slip closed at the touch. Then Elliott's fingers are gone, and he laughs as he darts to the bathroom, yelling as he shuts the door, "Dibs on first shower."

"One day, I'll stop falling for your tricks," Nico shouts back, and Elliott's response is muffled by the door and the sound of the running water, but Nico can still feel the warmth of his laughter in the pit of his stomach, filling him with pure, unadulterated joy.

RAYNA AND ELIZA come back two hours and fifteen minutes later with an ice cream cake and two large pizzas. As far as surprises go, it's not much of one at all. But Eliza's gaze darts between him and Elliott, upon their arrival, and a surge of satisfaction permeates the room when Elliott starts to blush under her scrutiny, confirming Nico's assumption this was all a ploy to give them some time alone. Eliza's cheeks are flushed, too, and Rayna's hair is a touch messier than it was when they left; Nico suspects they weren't the only ones taking advantage of their time spent away from one another.

They spend the rest of the night eating, and in the morning, Nico wakes to the sound of Eliza's laughter and Elliott's warm hand on his chest. It's the best vacation he's ever had, and he doesn't want it to end. He wants to stay suspended in this moment forever, never returning to the life of Santa's son. His only desire is to stay here in this hotel with his friends and his boyfriend and forget the responsibilities and expectations resting on his shoulders. This is the calmest he's felt in such a long time. He tries to catalog the feeling, bottle it up in a way he can tap into at a later date. He wants to save it for when he needs to be reminded of how things can be, of how things should be.

It's not until later, when Elliott has dropped him off at Noelle's house, Nico finally notices the appearance of silver in his hair. It's a stark contrast to his natural black, and while Nico's always known this would happen, it's surprising to see the shimmering metallic quality of the new strands mixed in. He's lying in bed, avoiding Noelle and Noah and their searching expressions as best he can. He's imagining how he'll look with a head full of silver hair and a beard to match, when there's a knock at his door. Nico doesn't answer, but he knows better than to think his silence will deter her.

She opens the door a beat later and settles onto the bed next to Nico, offering him a spoon. "Do you want some ice cream?"

She's resting the tub of ice cream on her large, round stomach and smiling at him around her own spoon. He shakes his head and she shrugs her shoulders, mumbling around her mouthful, "More for me, then."

They sit in amiable silence for a while, Nico enjoying the quiet comfort of Noelle's presence, and then Noelle finishes her ice cream and rests her head on Nico's shoulder, yawning, "How was your trip?"

Nico leans his head against Noelle's and sighs. He can't avoid telling her any longer. "I think I'm falling in love with Elliott."

"Mmm. Noticed the silver in your hair when you got home. Didn't know if I should say anything, though. Figured you'd bring it up if you wanted to talk about it. How long's it been there?"

"Not sure. Only now noticed it myself. It's been coming and going for a while now, though. Dad said it's essentially a magical side effect of falling in love. Comes and goes when I feel a strong emotion for Elliott. But I guess, since it's staying, that means something more."

"Do you think he's the one?"

"I-" he starts, then shuts his mouth to contemplate his answer. He's not let himself contemplate the future, not thoroughly anyway. He's been trying to focus on the now, how good things are with Elliott, and how warm and reassuring and steady the love growing inside him is. He knows it's happening. He knows what he's feeling, but he can't bring himself to accept it's real.

Noelle doesn't push him for an answer. The two of them sit there in silence and Noelle shows an astounding amount of patience as Nico thinks the question over.

"I think I'm almost ready to tell him I'm Santa's son," he says in answer. "For real this time."

Noelle sits up, looking Nico in the eyes, searching for something. She smiles, a slow, sweet thing and says very seriously, "That's big, Tico."

"I mean, I'm not ready yet, but I think— I don't know. I want to tell him, at least. I've never actually wanted to share this with anyone else. Not really. But maybe I'm getting overconfident things will work out because of the silvering hair. I honestly don't know."

Noelle's mouth turns down in a frown. "Oh, Nico, don't be like that."

"Be like what? I'm only being realistic."

"No, you aren't! You're being nervous and anxious. Which is fair. But I don't think being open to the idea of sharing this part of yourself with someone has anything to do with your hair! That's not—shit. That's not how any of this *works*. None of us fully understand how it does because it's magic, for fuck's sake, but I know your feelings for Elliott are causing this. All of it. Your magic, the Santa magic—it grows the more emotionally connected you are to someone, the deeper you care for them. That's how it's always been. Even entertaining the idea of sharing this information with Elliott is because of your emotions—because you care for him and trust him—not because your hair changed. Your hair *only* changed because of how you feel. You're falling in love—it's not overconfidence."

Nico thinks of Taylor and how sure he was he'd been the one. How his powers hadn't started to increase and how it made Nico think he should break it off. He doesn't want telling Elliott to be similar; he doesn't want to wonder if he did so on his own volition or if he was prompted by the Santa magic. He wishes he knew, without a doubt, he was making these decisions on his own.

"Look, I..."

"What's actually bothering you, Nico? What's going on?"

"Okay. Remember when I got here and I told you I ran into Taylor?"

"Yeah."

"Well I ran into him again on my first date with Elliott."

"And?"

"And I don't know! Is this all going too smoothly?"

"You're upset things are going well?"

Nico scrubs a hand over his face, frustration sinking in at how careful Noelle is being with her words. "No, of course not! I'm fucking ecstatic. But I have a suspicion the other shoe is eventually going to drop or something. I don't know! I loved Taylor. Or, I thought I did. But none of this ever happened when I was with him, and then I—well, you know—I ruined it. So I don't understand."

Noelle opens her mouth, shuts it, and then opens it again. She sighs and purses her lips and then finally speaks, "When you ran into him, what happened?"

"Nothing. He's engaged. I met his fiancé. That's it."

"Do you—" She starts and then she pauses, and Nico is hit with a rush of confusion before she begins again. "Are you still harboring feelings for him? Did you want to be the fiancé or something?"

"No," he says, sure as can be. "Honestly. No."

Her confusion spikes; he can feel it in his chest now. "Then I don't understand."

"Never mind, okay? Can we drop it already?"

"No, I don't think we can. It's obviously hindering your relationship with Elliott—or at the very least, making you doubt its validity when everything is going so well, and you shouldn't be."

Nico pinches the bridge of his nose and slumps back against the headboard, frustration rising like bile in his throat. "When I first saw him at the coffee shop the day I came here, I thought it was fate or something, you know? And then when I saw him again on my date with Elliott... Twice is too much to be a coincidence right? And I didn't feel anything. I wasn't jealous or disappointed he was marrying someone else, but I've thought about our breakup a lot over the years and how it changed the way I view this whole thing, and I think... I don't know. Maybe I keep running into him for a reason. It doesn't make sense for me to get my powers now, because of Elliott, when I was so sure Taylor was the one for me. None of this makes sense. I've known Elliott for less than half a year, and my hair's silvering, but I knew Taylor for four years, and *he loved me* and none of this happened. How does it make sense for it to be happening like it is?"

"Seems you're trying to find a way to undermine what you're feeling. Let's forget the magic. Forget the family business. Forget all of the expectations you have resting on your shoulders for a second. How do you feel about Elliott?"

"Good. Great. I care about him. I lo—" He cuts himself off, but Noelle's eyes widen at his slip. He swallows hard—he can't say it out loud yet—he's not ready.

"I *like* him a lot," he corrects. "A stupid amount."

Noelle reaches up and tousles Nico's hair, laughing, "Very eloquent."

She ignores his slipup, but Nico can recognize the surge of happiness lingering around them. It's been there since he almost said the word and Nico's not foolish enough to believe she'll forget his near-admission any time soon. "But seriously, Nico. If you don't want to be with Taylor, and you like Elliott a stupid amount, then I don't see what the problem is here."

"I guess there isn't one. I just don't understand."

Noelle rests her head on his shoulder again, continuing to card her fingers through his hair. "Of course you don't. It's magic."

After a long, deafening moment of silence, Nico says, barely above a whisper, "I guess I'm a little scared too."

Noelle wraps her arms around Nico and hugs him. "I know, love is terrifying sometimes."

Nico laughs into her hair. "I chickened out on telling Taylor because I could use all the magic not happening as proof it wasn't going to work out. But now this, now this is all happening, and it's clear *something* is going right, and I don't want—I don't want to mess it up. I don't want him to not want to be with me because of it. God, what if he doesn't want this life for himself?"

Noelle considers her response for a moment. She settles back against his shoulder and sympathetic understanding leaks out of her, washing over him in smooth, gentle waves. When Nico thinks she's not going to say anything, and that they're going to sit here in quiet comfort, she finally answers, "You won't know until you tell him...until you show him. I know it sucks. I wish I could just tell you it's all going to work out—and while I do believe that—I know you have to put your heart on the line to make it so."

"You're right," he laughs. "This does suck."

IT'S BEEN TWO weeks since he and Noelle talked through his feelings and he still hasn't been able to mention the subject of magic with Elliott. He wants to. He does. But then, every time he thinks he's found the right moment, he chickens out. They're on Elliott's couch, Nico lying with his head in Elliott's lap, and he thinks he's finally figured out the right way to broach the subject when Elliott scratches at his scalp and says, "So, my birthday's in three weeks."

"Don't remind me; time's going too fast. I'm still trying to get your gift together."

"Oh?" There's curiosity in his voice, but when Nico opens his eyes to see, it's not reflected on his face. There's a quiet thrum of nerves coming from him, instead, and Nico sits up, worried "You're nervous."

It's not a question but Elliott attempts to deny it, and Nico says, "No, Elliott. I know you are. I can feel it."

Everything seems to slow after Nico's confession. Elliott's nerves bubble up, turning giddy and infectious; they settle in Nico's heart and leave him tingling. Then Elliott's face transforms into something sweet and surprised and absolutely beautiful as he breathes out, "Oh."

"Yeah."

"I wasn't expecting that. I thought yours might be—"

Elliott's blushing and there's a fizzing sensation in Nico's fingers. These nerves are different than the ones before; there's a different current to them. It fills Nico with a warmth edging on too hot. He should tell Elliott more—this is his moment—but there's a lump in his throat, and he can't get the words out. He waits for Elliott to finish his thought, and when he does, Nico's chest could crack open with the force of his emotions.

"I thought yours had something to do with the elements. God, you hear stories, y'know, and sometimes when you touch me— This sounds ridiculous but at first I thought you must be running around nonstop with socks on or something because I've never met someone with so much static electricity. But sometimes, when you touch me, a shock goes up my entire body. Like—"

Nico reaches for his hand and when their palms meet, he feels it. The burst of electricity passing through them is more than it's ever been, and Elliott's eyes go wide. His emotions are hovering somewhere between disbelief and astonishment, and the bubbly, giddy feeling from before bursts inside Nico. "You have—you're— I've never met someone with cross-category powers."

Tell him. Tell him. Tell him.

He doesn't. Instead, he breathes "*Yeah*" against Elliott's mouth and gasps when the gentle hum of electricity goes from his lips to Elliott's as they kiss. Every point of contact is the same and soon Elliott pushes him back against the couch and places wet, sloppy kisses down his jaw and the column of his throat, nipping at the skin right above his collar. His pupils are blown, and his skin is flushed, and Nico desperately needs more contact, but Elliott pulls back and grins. Nico quirks an eyebrow in question and then Elliott laughs, surges forward and catches his mouth in another kiss.

When Nico pulls away for air, Elliott's eyes twinkle with mirth, and he says, punctuating each word with a kiss down his jaw, "This is quite electric."

Nico groans, but it turns into a soft gasp as Elliott scrapes his teeth over his skin. "Jesus, that was terrible."

Elliott's fingers pause at unbuttoning Nico's shirt, and he smirks at Nico when he whines, his smile only growing wider, more satisfied, when Nico says, "Don't tease."

"I'd never," Elliott huffs, in faux offense, but then he's making a show of taking his own clothes off, leaving Nico untouched, and it's hard to form sentences with the white-hot arousal coursing through his veins. Things have always been amplified like this, feeling his and his partner's arousal mix together and multiply within him while they're getting each other off. But this, this is something he's never experienced. This is all-encompassing, and every one of his nerves is lit up, and Elliott's not even touching him anymore. It's too much but not enough, and when Elliott hovers his hands over the buttons of Nico's shirt, he can't keep from whining, "Please, Elliott. Come on."

He smiles and starts undoing the buttons again, slowly and methodically, and Nico's begging, "Please, babe. *Please.*"

"Since you asked so nicely," Elliott breathes, and then he undresses him quickly, and their skin touches everywhere, and it's the best Nico's ever felt, and he never wants it to end. If he were a better person, he might have this revelation with his clothes on. But Elliott's touching him with a care bordering on reverence, and he can feel every single emotion Elliott has for him, from arousal to affection, burrowing its way into his heart and making a home and Nico *knows*. He knows this is who he wants to share his journey with.

"SO," NICO SAYS later, when they've both showered and are lying in Elliott's bed, legs tangling under the duvet, Nico's head resting on Elliott's chest. "You were mentioning your birthday earlier?"

Elliott's fingers trace a trail up Nico's arm, and he laughs. "Oh, yeah. My parents. They always do this outdoor party thing for my birthday. And, uh, yeah. I was wondering if you'd want to come."

"That's what you were nervous about?"

"Yeah, I don't know. Is meeting the parents too soon?"

Nico considers it. There's a steady uptick in his heartbeat as he does, because meeting the parents is a big deal in a lot of ways, but this is right. This is a safe situation to meet them in. They'll be surrounded by Elliott's friends and he won't be the sole object of his parents' attention. It's not too soon in the slightest. "Nah, I think it's good. Besides, you already met mine."

"That doesn't count," Elliott insists. "We weren't even dating yet."

"And whose fault was that?" Nico teases and Elliott's chest rumbles with laughter.

"Mmm. If I remember correctly, it was your sister, not mine. I—an only child—was not bringing any unprofessional complications to the table."

Nico snorts, pinching Elliott's stomach. "Oh shut up! She's in fourth grade! Who was going to think you were playing favorites?"

"Plenty of people could have," Elliott mumbles but his words hold no conviction. Nico picks up a slight tremor of embarrassment, right under the rush of amusement, and he glances up, waiting until Elliott meets his eyes to say, "It's cute. I liked how committed you were to it. To be honest, had it been me, I would've given in much sooner. Look at your face. How could I have resisted?"

Elliott scoffs, exaggerating a pout, "Is that all I am to you? A pretty face?"

"A pretty face and a wonderful mouth," Nico deadpans.

Elliott pushes at his cheek, laughing. "You are the worst and I hate you."

"No, you don't."

"No," Elliott says, giving him a quick kiss before pulling him in tighter against his chest. "I really, truly don't."

The feeling in his chest from earlier is back, warm and bright, telling him this is where he belongs. This is who he's supposed to be with. There's so much left to do. So much he still needs to tell Elliott, but he's starting to think it will be okay. He's starting to believe this is moving in the right direction and Elliott will accept him for who he is, and he won't be scared away by Santa's son.

Chapter Fourteen

"SO NICO, WHAT are your intentions with my dear Elliott?"

Eliza bursts out laughing, and Elliott groans into his hands. "Jesus, Willa, do you have to do this every time?"

There's an amused quality to his voice, so Nico knows he's not actually upset, but Willa's assessing him with steely blue eyes and Nico's intimidated. She's barely taller than Eliza, but she makes Nico feel small under her stare. She's got pale blonde hair and even fairer skin. She reminds him a little bit of Tinkerbell, attitude and all.

"Yes, Ellibaby. One heartbreak is enough for you."

Eliza giggles and stage whispers to Nico, "She makes it sound like she's not the one who broke his heart in the first place."

Nico's heart aches and his stomach drops. He was not expecting that. He assumed Willa was an old friend.

Elliott's laughing but he leans in to whisper to Nico, "Don't worry about her. We dated years ago, and things would have never worked out with us, anyway."

Willa gives Nico a sympathetic smile, as if she can guess what Elliott's told him, and explains, "Came as a real shock to Elliott when I told him I was a lesbian."

Eliza barks out a laugh, and Elliott dissolves into a fit of giggles next to him. Nico relaxes. Willa laughs, too, but a beat later, she says, "I'm serious, though. You hurt him, and I hurt you."

Elliott nudges his shoulder, whispering, "She's teasing," at the same time as someone says, "Willa dear, are you doing our jobs for us?"

A woman, who has Elliott's eyes, and a man, who looks like an older, blonder Elliott, join their group under the shade of the tree in the backyard, and Nico realizes these must be Elliott's parents.

"If you mean interrogating Elliott's new boyfriend, then yes. That is what she's doing," Eliza answers and everyone laughs, even Nico.

Elliott's mom sticks her hands out to grab Nico and pulls him in for a hug. "Oh we're only teasing. Elliott's told us so much about you. He's quite smitten."

"Mom!"

"Well you are," she says to Elliott before turning back to Nico. "He is. Anyway, I'm Linda, and this is my husband, David, and we're so glad to finally meet you. We were beginning to think Elliott was avoiding bringing you by."

"Honey, don't overwhelm him. They've not been dating too long."

David radiates fond exasperation from his emotions to his face. It puts Nico at ease. He knows they're teasing; he can't detect any lies in their words, but Willa's still watching him, and it's easy to feel like an intruder. But then Willa's face breaks into a smile and her eyes sparkle, and when she laughs, Nico lets out a breath he didn't know he was holding.

"Oh man, I like you, Nico. I've never seen someone so scared in my life. Elliott's last boyfriend didn't even pretend to take me seriously. He was a real ass of a rebound, babe."

Eliza and Linda nod in agreement, and Elliott blushes as David grimaces, "He was not your finest moment, son."

"Okay, okay. Can we go do cake and stop mentioning all my exes. You're all going to scare Nico away."

"They could never," Nico says, and he means to make it light and playful, but instead, it comes out serious and steady. Apparently it's very important for Elliott to know he's not going anywhere. If he's honest with himself, which he so rarely is, Nico knows it *is* important.

Eliza and Willa share a look, and Nico would have a hard time reading it if it weren't for the gush of protectiveness and acceptance passing through him. He knows he's said the right thing.

"Good," Elliott and his mother say at the same time. All Nico can feel is the overwhelming happiness surging through him as Elliott looks at him with a soft, small smile playing at his lips.

A beat later, Linda is ushering them all over toward the table on the porch where they've set a cake and a sizable pile of cards. There's a party hat in front of the cake Nico can only assume is meant for Elliott, by the way he groans, "Oh come on. We can't still be doing this."

Linda clucks her tongue. "You're not getting out of the party hats until you've got a family of your own to embarrass you on your birthdays. Until then, we're singing "Happy Birthday" while you wear this hat like always."

"We've been doing this since I was five," Elliott whines. Eliza loops her arm through Nico's, pulling him forward, her voice full of a gentle, fond teasing as she says to Nico, "It's delightfully ridiculous, and Elliott turns bright red every time. It's beautiful."

Elliott's already got a faint pink coloring his cheeks, which grows as his mom and Willa push him into the chair at the cake table. There are so many people around it's like the whole town is here, and they're all watching Elliott like they're waiting for a show. It turns out they are. There're trick candles and sparklers. Once they've sung "Happy Birthday" and the cake is cut, Eliza and Willa place one hand on each of Elliott's shoulders to keep him in place, and then together, with ear-to-ear smiles, they smash a piece of cake into his face. David waits with a towel and Elliott chuckles into it as he wipes the icing away. There are crumbs of cake and streaks of icing still in his hair, and he's adorable, face bright red but smiling as he thanks everyone for coming. The gaggle of people disperses from around the table, spreading out again throughout the backyard with their slices of cake.

His ability to read people's emotions is increasing with every day he spends with Elliott, their growing connection stimulating his latent powers, and it's odd to be surrounded by so many people and not be overwhelmed by all their different and conflicting feelings. He's starting to be able to tune them out, to turn it off when he doesn't want to experience them, which is a wonderful and welcome part of his growing magic. He's turned most of it off, but underneath it all, warm, gentle affection courses through the backyard, all directed at Elliott. It fills him with a bubbly sort of energy; he's so excited that, when they're finally given a moment to themselves, he picks up his card and shoves it in Elliott's hand.

"I thought you wanted me to open this when people weren't around?" Elliott asks, and Nico settles into the chair next to him, leaning forward and kissing him, quick and chaste.

"Changed my mind."

Nico's always been a perfect gift giver, one of the perks of the family line, but he still has a slight twinge of anxiety as Elliott opens the card and unfolds the papers inside.

Elliott's eyes widen, and his mouth falls open a bit. Nico's hit with a mixture of excitement and disbelief and awe. Elliott tears his gaze away from the papers, his eyes wide in shock as he stares at Nico. "These are floor seats. To see A. B. Cerise. At his sold-out show. In New York City."

"Yes," Nico agrees.

"Nico, how did you get these?" Nico senses a flicker of something close to embarrassment, and he doesn't understand until Elliott asks, "How much did you *pay* for these?"

Nico shrugs. "That doesn't matter. Honestly. I wanted to get them for you. You love him, and I have the money, and you've never been to New York, so I was thinking we'd make a weekend of it. I can show—"

His words are cut off by the force of Elliott's hug, and then Nico's being kissed all over his face while Elliott laughs between each one. "Thank you. Thank you. Thank you."

The knot of tension in Nico's chest eases, replaced with Elliott's excitement, and Nico knows he got the right gift.

THE LAST DAYS of May bleed away, and then Nico blinks and he's busier than ever before. He's started picking up more of Noelle's responsibilities around Kahveci's so she doesn't have to be on her feet as much as her due date approaches. Soon, it's mid-June, and she's overdue. Nico's now at the coffee shop from open to close, giving Noah time to be with Noelle since she could go into labor at any moment, and though Elliott's schedule is almost entirely cleared because school's let out, they only get to spend any quality time together at night after Nico locks up. He's all but living with Elliott now. It's not a big deal, and he tells Eliza as much when she comes by to ask him about his new living arrangements while she orders her coffee.

It's only convenience. It's so much easier to walk upstairs to Elliott's bed when he's tired from a long day at the coffee shop than it is to go all the way back to his own. It's easy to start falling into the habit, as his all-day shifts get more frequent, to eventually spend every night at Elliott's place once Noelle is past due and relying heavily on Nico to be the backbone of the shop, so Noah can be home with her. It's easy, but it's also nice.

It's nice to wake up next to Elliott in the morning. He's not allowed himself to consistently spend a night in another man's bed for years, and he loves it, loves the warmth along his back, and Elliott's arm curling around him, hugging him close. He loves the way Elliott mumbles his goodbyes, half asleep as Nico leaves in the early morning hours, how he comes by the coffee shop just to say hello, how his face lights up every night as Nico walks through the door.

It's good in a way Nico thinks nothing has ever been before, in a way he never wants to end. It's not a big deal to be staying at Elliott's place every night; he truly doesn't think it is, no matter what Noelle and Eliza say, but one day he wakes up with a full head of silver hair, and he realizes it's a far bigger deal than he imagined it to be.

He'd known for a while he was falling in love. He noticed it build with each moment more he spent with Elliott, felt the gentle thrum of affection, which had carved its place in his heart, growing whenever Elliott was around. Still, he didn't want to admit it, didn't want to be the first one to say it. Now though, while he examines a full head of shimmering silver hair in the mirror, it's hard to deny—he's in love and he's going to have to tell Elliott.

Chapter Fifteen

NICO LEAVES FOR the morning shift as he always does. Elliott kisses him goodbye from the bed, eyes barely open, voice rough with sleep, and he doesn't notice the hair. Nico has the day to figure out how he'll tell him everything, how he'll break the family secret to him. Somewhere between making a drink wrong three times in a row, he decides it's best to ease Elliott into things. He already knows he has multiple types of powers, but now he's going to have a very obvious indication Nico possesses even more magic than he's let on. He'll start with the basics, tell him he's Santa's son—make him believe when he hadn't before. If that goes well, he'll tell him the other things too: how the Santafication process relies on a bond of love, how their commitment to each other is bound with magic, how he doesn't fully become Santa Claus until his father retires and the ceremonial Passing of the Hat takes place. How, at its core, the continuation of the Santa line rests entirely on whether or not Elliott feels the same for, and wants to spend his life with, Nico.

It's a lot to take in. Nico's lived with the information his entire life, and it's still a lot to wrap his mind around. He can't imagine being in Elliott's position and not taking it poorly, but he has to hope it goes well. He hopes if he tells Elliott a little at a time, shows him the things he can do, he'll at least believe the Santa part. If Elliott believes that, Nico can worry about the rest later.

As Addison arrives for her shift, Nico gets a call from Noah to inform him Noelle has gone into labor. He doesn't experience people's emotions over the phone, but the excitement in Noah's voice still settles into Nico's stomach with a fizzing sensation. It distracts him the rest of the day. He's so excited Noelle's going to be a mother he almost forgets what he was planning to tell Elliott when he drops by as he and Addison are closing. But then Elliott's face twists in confusion, and it all comes crashing back to him, the nerves replacing the excitement in an instant.

"Your hair," is all he says, and Addison turns on the spot, chiming in excitedly, "Aha! Your boyfriend's here, so there's no way of getting out of an explanation. Spill."

"Hey, Addy," Nico says, not wanting to have this conversation with another party involved. "You can leave. I can finish up here."

Her face and her emotions flash between relief and disappointment and then back to relief in a split second. She unties her apron and laughs, shaking her head as she does. "Hey, if you want to let me go early instead of explaining how your sweet hair is a premature midlife crisis thing then so be it. I'm not complaining."

Elliott smiles, his amusement coursing through Nico and dampening the offense he's feeling. Nico doesn't sound nearly as affronted as he would have if he wasn't being affected by Elliott's emotions. "It's not a midlife crisis! I'm not even thirty yet!"

She waves a hand from the door and smiles, her voice saccharine, "Whatever you say, Nic. See you tomorrow!"

The moment the door clicks closed Elliott says, "So. I assume this is a magic thing since you didn't want to say it in front of Addison."

"Yeah."

"But you already told me about the feelings, and I know—" He stops short, face burning bright red. He clears his throat. "And I know about the elements. I— You can change your appearance too? I've never— Babe, how many powers do you have?"

Nico tries to turn it off, he tries not to feel what Elliott's feeling, but it's too strong. There's an overwhelming awe washing over him and no. This isn't the response he wanted. "No, that's not. I'm not. I don't have cross-categorical power. I'm not that special."

A rising tide of confusion. A furrowed brow. Pursed lips. "I don't understand. I've literally felt your— I've felt the electricity. And you told me—you said you know what I'm feeling. You said that."

"I did. I know."

Elliott's upset. It boils furiously in Nico's stomach, the pain and confusion exploding through his esophagus like acid. "Then I don't understand. You obviously have magic from different categories! Heart and Exterior! That's two! And don't tell me you dyed your hair because no one can obtain an actual metallic quality without Body magic. I am not an idiot, Nico."

His voice is too loud in the quiet coffee shop, and Nico knows he's made a huge mistake.

"I know you're not. I don't think you are. I—"

He's trying to find the right words to explain, but Elliott cuts him off, his voice a quiet plea. "Why are you lying to me, Nico?"

Nico wipes a hand over his face and looks at Elliott, desperate for him to understand, but not knowing how to tell him when they've started off on the wrong foot. "I'm not lying to you. I do not have cross-categorical magic in the way you're thinking. You have to believe me. I'm telling the truth.

I really am. It's—my family's magic is a little complicated. Different than everyone else's."

"Okay, then tell me."

His voice still has a bit of an edge to it, but the hurt has largely subsided, and Nico sighs in relief. "Okay. I will. Of course. Give me a minute to finish up here? We can talk upstairs if that's okay?"

"Yeah, okay. I'll—yeah. I'll see you up there. I'm going to— Yeah."

Nico wasn't expecting him to stay while he finished closing the shop, but Elliott's absence, and the way he left, puts Nico on edge. He closes quicker than ever before, and though he'll regret it in the morning, right now all he wants is to get to Elliott and fix this before it gets out of hand.

Once upstairs, he dawdles in the living room, the desire to get to Elliott as soon as possible tapering off the moment he realizes Elliott isn't waiting on the couch for him. Elliott's in his room, sitting on his bed with his head tilted back against the headboard, staring up at the ceiling. He's much calmer than he was in the coffee shop, and Nico closes the door to alert him he's there.

"That was quick," he says by way of greeting.

Nico laughs; it's flat and forced, though. "Yeah, wanted to explain. Sooner rather than later. I mean, it's already later than I should have. But you know what I mean."

Elliott's mouth quirks at the corners, and Nico's nerves spike. He doesn't want him to revert back to being upset; he wants to make him smile in full. He hopes he takes this well.

"Okay first let me be upfront. Noelle's in labor and she has been for hours, and honestly, Noah could call at any moment to tell me the baby's here, so I wanted you to know because, if I check my phone, it's not because I'm not taking this conversation seriously. Okay?"

Elliott's smile grows a fraction and a flare of affection hits Nico. Elliott's words are soft, but his face barely betrays the fondness Nico knows he's feeling. "Of course. I understand. And you— If you want to go over to the hospital, this can wait. We can talk later."

"Nah, no. Hate waiting rooms, and I can't imagine Noelle would want me in there with them. Actually, I know she wouldn't. She'd definitely bite my head off for even suggesting I intrude on her and Noah's moment."

Elliott laughs, softly and quietly, but the joy is there, and Nico is starting to feel more settled. "Okay. You have my full attention, then. I'd love to hear what's happening."

Nico joins Elliott on the bed, sitting at the corner until Elliott pats the spot next to him and says, "Don't be like that. Come on."

Elliott calling him over is good. He's at least not upset enough to not want to be near him. Their shoulders knock as Nico settles in next to him, and Elliott leans into the touch. Nico feels warm and confident. He can do this.

"Do you remember Chrysanthemum's parent-teacher conference?"

"Yes?" Elliott leans away from Nico so he can see his face, and Nico wishes, not for the first time, Elliot was the one who could feel emotions. He wishes he could make Elliott understand he's telling the truth without having to rely solely on his words. It'd be so much easier for him to just know, like Nico does, when someone is honest. Instead, Nico takes a deep breath and barrels on.

"I told you I was Santa's son and Chrys was my elf supervisor, right? Yeah! Don't give me that look! I'm not— I know you think I was joking. I know it's absurd! No one believes in Santa Claus. We're in a world full of magic but myths? No deal, right? It's how people think. There's a limit to what we can believe even though we literally have magic coursing through us. That's how it— Please, let me finish before you say anything, or I might not be able to go through with this."

Elliott closes his mouth and nods, letting Nico continue uninterrupted. "Anyway. That's how it is when we— Actually, no. This is what gets passed down in our family. I've never told anyone this— You're the first person outside my family I've ever seriously considered telling. So yeah, I don't know if people believe in myths, but not a lot of people say Santa Claus is real, and then I told you, and you obviously didn't believe me. So, it confirmed all my concerns. I immediately thought: 'See, people will never believe me; they'll always think I'm pulling their leg.' Which, I mean, I—"

Elliott touches his hand, fingers twining with Nico's, and he squeezes. "Can I ask you something?"

"Yeah," Nico says around a lump in his throat. There's so much more to say, but he can't quite put the words together, so maybe it will help if he explains based on Elliott's questions instead.

"Is Chrysanthemum your sister?"

Nico is so taken aback by the question he laughs, the sound ripping through him and he can't stop, can't compose himself, as Elliott's affection courses through him. "That's the first thing you're going to ask?"

"I take that as a no, then."

"No, she actually is an elf. She was sent here to watch over me and keep me on track, but well, I was into you, and you didn't want to date me if she was my sister so her being here fucked everything up. Which, I do owe you for in the end. I think this is the first time I've ever seen my father admit he was wrong. You really brought us together on that one."

Embarrassment. Confusion. Affection. So much affection. A drop of pride. Amusement. Elliott's experiencing so much and his voice brims with emotion as he says, "Glad I could help. You don't talk about your dad very much, but I get the feeling you're not as close with him as the rest of your family. I'm— It's nice something good came out of my stupidity."

"First, I didn't exactly set it up to where you could believe me. Noelle says I presented it as a joke. Which I guess I did. I don't blame you for not believing me. It would have been a miracle if you had." He pauses, pressing a quick kiss against Elliott's mouth and sighs into it when Elliott kisses him back.

He pulls away a moment later, knowing they need to finish this conversation before they get lost in the touch of each other. "You believe me?"

Elliott considers it for a moment, and Nico can tell he's mulling over his answer. "Yeah, I do. I mean, it's definitely a lot to take in, and I have so many questions, and I can't believe it, but I do believe it, y'know. Santa Claus is real, and I'm in love with his son. It should be unbelievable but..."

Nico's brain whites out, his thoughts crashing to a stop at Elliott's admission.

"You love me?" Nico asks at the same time Elliott reaches for Nico's face and rubs a finger over his jaw, voice full of awe as he says, "Your beard."

"What—"

"Wait, my beard?"

"Oh god, I said that out loud—"

Nico touches his face. There was only a five o'clock shadow when he left the coffee shop, but now, there's a close-cropped beard covering his jaw. He's in awe, but more so by Elliott's confession than anything else.

"You love me," he says, and he knows. He knows it's true. The beard, the way his chest swells with warmth, not his own, the look in Elliott's eyes—they all let Nico know those three words are true even before Elliott answers, "Yeah, I do."

"You love me," he repeats, still so shocked. "And you believe me?"

"Yes." Elliott smiles, pulling Nico in to settle against his side. He presses a kiss to the top of his head and says, "I do. I really, truly do."

"Good, good. Yeah, really good. That's good." It's overwhelming. His head is spinning with the force of Elliott's emotions thrumming through him, tangling with his own. It's mesmerizing. His body feels like it's been wrapped in warm, plush fabric, soft and gentle and protective. "I wish I could tell you how this feels. I can't explain it; different emotions feel different on the inside. But with you, when you're happy. God, it's so overwhelming. I can feel it all over, it's honestly so much. It's like no one else. No one else's happiness overwhelms my senses the way yours does."

"I think— yeah. That's got to be because my happiness is infectious. Literally."

Nico leans back so he can see Elliott's face. He seems a little nervous, and Nico only has a moment to wonder before Elliott's explaining, "Eliza knows. Willa, of course. My parents, obviously. But I don't—tell a lot of people. You know how it is."

"Yeah," Nico sighs. He ducks his head back against Elliott's shoulder, snuggling in. "I do. I've actually—" He cuts himself off with a nervous laugh. "A lot of people have told or shown me theirs but when it came time to tell you, when I thought, 'oh this'll never get off the ground if I don't tell him,' because Chrys was here, which was a disaster. But I— I clammed up. Couldn't tell you when I barely knew you. It's so—"

"Intimate," Elliott supplies.

"Yeah," Nico agrees. "But I love you, and it feels right to share this with you now."

Elliott laughs, body relaxing beside Nico. "For a second, I thought you weren't going to say it back."

Nico turns his face, angling up for a kiss and Elliott obliges. Nico smiles as he pulls away and says, "Have to keep you on your toes."

Elliott hums. "Of course, for sure."

They fall into a comfortable silence until the high of the moment starts to wear off and Nico begins to worry about all the things he still needs to divulge, needs to explain.

"There's actually—" Nico clears his throat, nervous again.

Elliott runs his fingers through Nico's hair, soothing. Nico takes a deep breath and starts again, hoping Elliott will understand. "There's actually a lot more I need to tell you. More than the powers and shit. There's a lot of family obligations and ceremonies and—"

Elliott reaches around and puts his fingers under Nico's chin, pulling his face upward so they're eye to eye again. "You can take your time. I— Hell, I didn't even tell you what my power is until today even though you—you— I mean you *Displayed your*s for me and you've never said anything. Or even asked. You've been very patient. So I can wait. I don't need to know all about it right now."

"I appreciate it. I'm going to tell you, though. But I need some time first. I don't want to throw it all on you right now and freak you out."

"I'm not. I won't. But I understand you want to wait. That's totally cool."

Nico can tell Elliott is convinced what he's saying is true, and Nico wants to accept him at his word. He wants to believe once he reveals the stipulations of being Santa's son Elliott won't feel differently. But the trick to knowing a future promise is the truth, is realizing there's no way Elliott can know for sure without being presented with all the facts. So Nico smiles, presses a kiss to Elliott's cheek, and hopes like hell it all works out. He wants this so badly; he can't imagine how crushed he'll be after allowing himself a taste of what love feels like if it all comes crashing down.

Chapter Sixteen

NOELLE'S AND NOAH'S daughter is born one minute before midnight on the twenty-second of June. Noelle's birthday is the next day, and when Nico visits her in the hospital, she says it's the best gift she's ever received. He's never seen his sister so happy—she's radiant. The following week at the coffee shop is the busiest he's ever seen. It's like everyone in town stops by at least once to tell Nico to send their regards to Noelle, and at least half of them arrive with care packages to go along with their well wishes. Winnie and Jan even stop by with what appears to be an entire wardrobe of baby clothes for Nadia.

His family arrives as July begins. The first to visit are his parents. His mom tells him he's handsome with silver hair the moment she sees him, but Kristoff doesn't acknowledge it. He doesn't even mention Santa or the countdown being halfway through until the week is over and they're leaving. He takes Nico aside and tells him he's proud of him, he's happy for him, and he's excited he's so close to fulfilling his duties as heir. It leaves him with a sense of confidence he didn't have before. He's in love, his powers are strengthening with every passing day, and his father's proud of him. It's everything he's always wanted but told himself he didn't.

Joy and Eloise come next. Hattie and Collette split their time fawning over Nadia and interrogating Elliott. He takes it in stride, and when they leave, he jokes the twins were more intimidating than Kristoff. Afterward, Carol and Jay come with Timmy. They offer the chillest visit of all. But as they leave, Elliott tells him, with a grin, Timmy threatened to put him in time-out forever if he hurt Nico. Then, Belle and Henrik come with their three children, and Nico's never been happier Elliott welcomed him into his apartment as if it was nothing—Noelle's house is too busy with all those people around.

With the onslaught of family, it's easy for Nico to get distracted, but once they're gone, and things slow down, the reality of the situation hits him like a sack of bricks. It's been six weeks since he shared with Elliott he's Santa's son, and he still hasn't even broached the subject of what it entails. Elliott has been true to his word and hasn't brought it up, perfectly fine to wait for Nico to tell him. But Nico can't; he shuts down anytime he even imagines sharing any more of the family secrets with Elliott. He doesn't want to ruin how good things have become—how easy it's been to make a home out of Elliott's apartment—by informing him there's a deadline nearing. He doesn't want to disclose that the last and final prerequisite for taking on the Santa name is a mutual and lifelong commitment to each other. He's not sure marriage is on the table yet, and he doesn't want to tell Elliott it's essentially what's needed and freak him out.

This isn't how things are supposed to be. He should be able to propose on his own time, or let Elliott propose—it seems he'd want to be the one—not because some magical force is relying on him to do so by the Christmas of his thirtieth year. He hates this. He's been coming around to the idea—the cold, bitter resentment he's felt for so long is thawing into a reluctant acceptance. Now, though, as time marches forward and the deadline approaches more and more quickly, the negativity comes back to him almost as strong as it was before. His life is out of his control: his love life is being dictated by someone else; his existence, in general, is just a cog in a wheel of Santa history, and it doesn't matter what he actually wants.

Two weeks later, when Noelle invites him over, with the stipulation to leave Elliott behind, she demands to know what's been going on with him lately, and he shares his turmoil.

She sighs. "Listen, Nico. I think you've got to rip the Band-Aid off and tell him. You're in love. He's in love. You're living together—" She holds her hand up when he starts to protest, and he shuts his mouth.

"I am too exhausted to deal with your bullshit, okay? Nadia's been keeping me up, and on top of that, I've been worried because you were doing so well. You were so happy, and now you're sullen again. And I know it sucks. I know it all fucking sucks. It's absurd how this is quite literally out of your hands at this point. You've done what you can. You fell in love; now you've got to wait. See how it pans out. See if he'll commit. But he can't commit if you don't share with him what's on the line—if you don't even tell him what committing to you entails. That's not— Nico, that's not fair to him."

"I know, okay? I know! But I don't want to tell him everything and have him feel pressured to be with me, or whatever, before he's ready?"

"I mean, you're already together. You're sleeping together. You're living together. You love each other. There's not—"

"It's a lifelong commitment, Noelle! I'm not—marriage! That's what it is. Am I—is he—are we even ready to put *marriage* on the table? Because I'm not sure we are."

Noelle nods, contemplative. "You don't have to get married on Christmas. Do you? I mean, how's it work anyway? How do you know when the Santafication is over?"

Nico buries his head in his hands, groaning in frustration. "Dad says you just know."

"Oh yeah," Noelle snorts. "Really clears things up all right."

Nico shrugs. "He said there'd be some glowing. I can't tell if he was being serious or not."

"Has Dad ever joked a day in his life?"

"Well you're not wrong there!" Nico laughs, but it's hollow. He's not very amused.

"Well...has there been any glowing?"

"Would I be in this situation if there had been?"

"I guess not."

Silence lapses between them, Nico feeling marginally better after getting some of his anxieties off his chest, and then Noelle asks something, causing them to well back up. "So, let's be honest here. You don't want to tell him all this stuff because you want the glowing, or whatever the hell happens, to occur first? Before you have to?"

Nico's heartbeat quickens and his stomach swoops. She's always had a way of striking right to the core and figuring him out.

"Ah, I see," Noelle says a moment later. "You want to have the magic confirm it's real—the commitment's been made—without having to talk."

"I—" She gives him a sharp, disapproving look and he falters. "Okay, yeah. Maybe that's it."

Noelle mulls it over for a bit, and then she gets up and checks on Nadia sleeping in the bassinet by the window. It's not until she's settled back on the couch with her feet tucked underneath her that she levels Nico with a no-nonsense glare and says, "You're an idiot! You're being dumb as hell. You can't build a marriage—and that's what this will eventually be if it all works out—without being completely honest. And you don't want to tell him becoming Santa relies on him too? That it's not just you? That's a hell of a secret to keep."

"I want to tell him! I just don't—" He scrubs his hand over his face, as if it will clear his head of some of his anxiety. "I'm going to tell him. I'm—we have our trip next week. The concert tickets I got him for his birthday? We leave on Sunday if you don't ne—"

"Don't you dare try to cancel your trip because of me! You've helped out so much this year, especially the last few months, and Noah and I are eternally grateful, but we have it covered. And if what you're trying to say is you're telling him on your trip then I am absolutely going to change the locks at Kahveci's if you so much as *consider* coming into work instead of going."

"You wouldn't."

Noelle raises an eyebrow.

"Okay, you might."

"Exactly. Don't test me," she says, smirking. Then her face softens and she continues, much gentler this time, "Go show off your apartment. Enjoy yourself. Tell Elliott. I honestly think it'll make you feel better."

SUNDAY COMES AND Nico fully expects Elliott to freak out on the plane by the amount of complaining he does leading up to the flight. But all he does is clasp Nico's hand at takeoff, holding on a little shy of too tight. On the descent he doesn't even grab Nico's hand; instead, he's laughing and relaxed, and Nico categorizes the flight as a success. When they get off at the stop closest to Nico's apartment, he's suddenly filled with nerves and jitters. He doesn't know why; it doesn't make sense when they've been living together for months, but the idea of bringing Elliott into his home—his actual home—makes him feel strung tight, ready to snap. This is the place he carved out and made his own despite the needling voice in the back of his mind telling him he was only delaying the inevitable; he'd eventually have to go home—to upstate New York and the portal to the Northern Realm.

Letting Elliott into this part of his life is another form of intimacy. So instead, Nico takes Elliott through Central Park, delaying the inevitable for a moment longer. He knows he's being ridiculous. Elliott's already aware of so much, and it's not like showing him the inside of his apartment is going to change anything. But it feels like it will cement something Nico's not convinced he can—or should—have.

They walk hand in hand through the park, and Nico watches Elliott as he takes everything in. Elliott slows as he sees two men in the distance swinging a small boy, shrieking with laughter, between their arms. Elliott's face is wistful, and there's a soft longing curling through him, and Nico knows, before he asks, but he needs to hear it from Elliott himself.

"Do you want kids?"

"Yeah, definitely," Elliott answers automatically. He's thoughtful for a moment, a bubbling of nerves spiking through him and into Nico, and then he adds, "I actually want to adopt."

He turns his face to Nico then, eyes bright and determined. "Even if—even if I were with someone who could get pregnant, I'd still want to adopt."

Nico can hear his heart beating in his ears, and he has to concentrate on Elliott's voice to drown out the rising panic bubbling up in his own chest. He's not even sure if adoption is on the table for them. As far as he knows, there have always been biological heirs and he doesn't know how they'll get around it—he wasn't even convinced surrogacy would work at first. But Elliott is so sure, the fierceness with which he says his next words illustrates how important this is to him, and Nico knows he's going to need to make adoption work if he wants this to last.

"I know there are different ways for queer couples to have kids now, and I know having biological children is important to some people. But, my mom's adopted, and Willa had a shitty time in foster care before she—before her parents adopted her, and it's really important to me. To adopt. To help as many children, as I can, find a home."

"That's really—" His heart is aching. He's never considered children before, not outside the heir, but now—now he can't imagine anything other than adopting. "I love that idea."

Elliott quirks an eyebrow. His face is otherwise impassive, but there's a spark of excitement coursing through Nico's veins he knows isn't his own. "Oh?"

"Yeah I've never thought—I mean, my dad puts a lot of—God. I—" Nico huffs out a laugh, all air and not amused in the slightest. "I actually came out to my family this Christmas. The whole, Santa thing. There're some expectations, and I—well, you know how it goes, or, you know how it can go. I know your parents have always been supportive, and well, Joy's a lesbian, and I guess I should have known, but I—"

Elliott grabs his hands and rubs his thumb over Nico's knuckles. The touch soothes him, and Nico sighs in relief, continuing. "Anyway, there's always been some expectations for me when it comes to getting married and producing an heir—"

Elliott's gaze shoots up and Nico's laugh escapes him; there's more amusement in it this time.

"Yeah," Nico says, agreeing with Elliott's unspoken bewilderment, "It sounds a lot like a fucking kingdom, and it's stressed me out for years. I know. Anyway, I've always thought adoption would be out, but I like the idea of adopting. Helping kids who need homes. I'd— Yeah. I'd love to do that, actually."

Bright, hot happiness bursts through him and then it slows, creeping over him at a soft, soothing pace. Elliott's emotions are always so much stronger than anyone else's, but this, this is overwhelming and calming at the same time. He's at peace discussing children in a way he never has been before, in a way he never could have imagined before meeting Elliott.

Elliott's smile is all-encompassing, his eyes are bright with it as he croaks out, "You want to adopt because I want to adopt."

"Yeah, I do."

"You want to adopt children with me."

Commitment. It's all he can think, heart hammering away in his chest, the sound deafening in his ears. "Yeah, I do."

The words hang in the air between them for a moment that stretches far too long for Nico's liking. He worries he's said too much, but then Elliott squeezes his hand, his smile growing impossibly wide. "Good. Good, yeah. I want that too."

Nico sighs in relief, body relaxing. There's no glowing and he doesn't feel any different. He doesn't *know* if the process is done, but discussing children, planning for the future together in the middle of Central Park—damn, if it doesn't feel like a step in the right direction for Nico.

SOON ENOUGH, THE discomfort of walking around with a duffle bag digging into his shoulder outweighs his nerves and Nico brings Elliott back to his apartment. Nico unlocks the door, holds it open for Elliott to cross the threshold first, and waits with bated breath, hoping Elliott will think it's nice.

Elliott sets his bag at the door and stays put, never fully stepping inside the apartment, and Nico's too anxious to walk around him to see his face. He's so nervous he doesn't even want to experience Elliott's emotions with him. But he's having to concentrate as hard as he can to not feel any of them and even still, there's a subtle thrumming sensation coursing through him. The emotion is muted, but even then there's bubbly intensity to it.

"You know," Elliott starts, turning toward him, dragging Nico out of his concentration. His walls slip and the nervous energy Nico now recognizes Elliott has been feeling, hits Nico like a freight train. It knocks the breath out of him and all he can think as Elliott continues is *Please don't hate it.*

"I knew, vaguely, you were loaded. I mean, the floor seats for A. B.? And this whole trip, and you're always getting me things, which I love, obviously, but I know it adds up. So I knew, of course. Your sister has a house *and* a giant garage apartment you don't pay rent for. And she owns a coffee shop. I mean, an extremely nice, well-visited coffee shop, and I know Pine Cove's cost of living isn't—anyway. I had a vague understanding you and your sister came from money. And I know I've never been to New York; hell, I've barely even been outside of Maine, but I know Central Park's an expensive area, right? I don't know what I'm saying,"

Elliott trails off, laughing. He runs a hand over his face, still nervous, and Nico can hear his heartbeat in his ears again. He'd never thought of taking Elliott here in that way. He never realized what it might look like to Elliott, a small-town boy, who's never been on a plane, to see up-close how Nico lives when he isn't in Pine Cove. He never hid his money; as Elliott said, he gives him gifts, shows him he cares with novelty items priced too high to be reasonable, but the cost didn't matter when he had the money and Elliott liked them. So no, he never hid his money. But he didn't want to flaunt it, not in a way someone could interpret as "I have a gross amount of money. Please love me." He hopes Elliott's never read it as anything but "I have this and I want to spend it on you because I can and I love you." It never occurred to him Elliott might be put off by it. Now? Well...

"I hope," Elliott finally says, interrupting Nico's rapid descent into panic. "I mean, I like it. The apartment's nice. But I hope, I know we've never discussed your family in *too much* detail, and I guess that's probably because, for a while, you couldn't tell me anything real. And, yeah. Anyway, what I'm trying to say, and what's suddenly concerning me, is I hope you didn't think you had to hide your money from me? Like, I'd think of you differently if I knew how rich you were. Or it'd change my perception of you or something. I'm not going to treat you differently or want more from you, or I don't know! It all sounds dumb because I've never felt this way until *right now* but I—knowing you have a lot of money isn't going to—it doesn't change anything?"

It comes out a question, almost a plea, like he needs confirmation from Nico and all Nico can see is the desperation in Elliott's eyes as he said he wasn't going to want more from him and what he must mean.

"Okay first, let's get this straight right now: it never once crossed my mind I needed to keep my money from you in an attempt to not get played or something? That wasn't on my mind at all. Ever."

Relief washes over Nico in waves as Elliott's eyes soften and his shoulders relax.

Elliott sighs. "Yeah, I didn't really think." His mouth turns down in a deprecating kind of way, and he huffs out a laugh. "You already spend enough on me, and I love it because I know you love doing it, and honestly, who doesn't love gifts? But now seems as good a time as any to be clear I'm not—I've never expected those things, and I'm not going to expect anything different now that you've brought me here. Shown me this part of you."

Nico sighs, his own relief mixing with Elliott's to make him light-headed and floaty. They stand there in silence for a moment, and then Elliott raises an eyebrow, his voice only giving away a fraction of the hope Nico knows he feels as he asks, "So this doesn't change anything?"

"God, no!" Nico laughs. "No, this doesn't change anything. At all. I mean, well I guess it sort of changes things but in a good way. Now we're sharing even more with each other. I know you want to adopt and now you've seen my apartment in New York that I use as a hideout from my problems and my father. And you like it? I hope you like it because I was afraid you wouldn't like it, which doesn't make any sense because it's an apartment. And with how much I travel it's nothing like you letting me move into your place. But it's still my home, and I know my whole life is basically funded by my father, but this is mine, y'know? I decorated, and I picked it out, and it's where I've made a home and you're—God, I love you. And I want you to appreciate my things."

Elliott smiles and walks forward, closing the small gap between the two of them. He settles his hands against Nico's hips, pulling him in for a hug. His smile grows slowly, fondly as he waits for Nico to wrap his arms around his neck. Then he asks, with a glint in his eyes and laughter in his voice, "You thought I could do anything but love this big, beautiful, wonderful insight into who you are, who you were before I knew you?"

"Well when you put it like that it sounds ridiculous," Nico tries to pout, but the warmth of Elliott's body pressed against his and the slow, steady thrum of his happiness coursing through his veins undermines the effect.

His put-upon frown is even wiped off his face as Elliott says, "You should give me a tour. Show me what Nico Hamurişi is all about."

There's a glint in his eyes and a rush of heat beating down on Nico telling him the bedroom should be last. He takes Elliott's hand and pulls him forward, voice lilting as he says, "Follow me, darling."

Chapter Seventeen

THEY DON'T LEAVE the apartment the first day. Truthfully, they barely leave Nico's room the whole day, not coming out until later when the sun is starting to fade and their stomachs are starting to grumble. They order food and put a movie on, but Elliott's long since given up trying to get Nico to pay attention to a movie, especially when they're alone. As expected, Nico doesn't know what the movie is about or even what the title is, but by the end, Elliott's sprawled out on top of him, breath ghosting against his neck as he dozes off, and Nico knows, for sure, he's happier than he's ever been.

They spend the next four days being tourists. Elliott's never been to New York, and while Nico's already visited all the major attractions several times over, he wants nothing more than to show Elliott all the wonders of the city. Each day he goes through multiple scenarios of how to tell Elliott everything being the heir to the Santa line entails, all the obligations and expectations, but every night, when they return to his apartment, Nico balks.

The day of the concert—the thing that brought them here, the thing Nico's been working so hard to make special for Elliot—is the most overwhelming experience Nico's had in some time. Elliott can't stop moving and Nico can feel all that raw, excited energy coursing through him and hiking up the beat of his already racing heart. Elliott's excitement is contagious, and it's always so intense for Nico, to be able to feel emotions and have the good ones amplified tenfold because of Elliott's own power. He doesn't think he's ever going to get used to it: the white-hot energy warming his entire being every time Elliott is near him and happy. It's intoxicating.

Outside of Elliott's emotions, there are Nico's own nerves ratcheting up his heartbeat and adrenaline. By the time they get on the subway to Madison Square Garden, he's so keyed up he might burn right out of his skin.

"So about tonight," Nico starts, and Elliott's attention snaps to his. It throws Nico off balance for a moment, makes his nerves flare the tiniest bit, but he knows they shouldn't. This is something good, something Elliott will like. He knows he doesn't need to be worried he won't. Elliott will be ecstatic over the last-minute addition to the gift. He's sure of this, and yet he still trips over his words, "I, uh, didn't want to tell you when I gave you the tickets in case I couldn't make it happen or it fell through or something. But yeah, before the concert—I arranged—I mean, yeah. We're meeting him. A. B."

Elliott's eyes go impossibly wide, and Nico makes a point of blocking out some of Elliott's feelings, concentrating on letting himself feel those of the people around them as well to counteract the sheer force of Elliott's excitement hitting him. "Wait! You're kid—oh my god, oh my god. You can't be serious." He touches his mouth in shock, blinking rapidly back at Nico. "How?"

Nico's cheeks are burning. "Oh, I know a guy." *Slept with a guy.* "From a photo job." *A groomsman.* "We kept in touch a bit over the years." *Hooked up when we could.* "He's a crew member for the tour, and he owed me a favor." *He puked in my car the last time I saw him.* "Though, I thought this would definitely be too big to make happen but—"

Nico shrugs his shoulders, letting a bit more of Elliott's excitement seep into him, surging him forward, "Apparently A. B. does a raffle or something? A random drawing of tickets so people don't have to pay extra to meet him, so it's fairer. Or, I assume that's why, but anyway, it didn't take much to convince him, I guess. Rafael says he's super friendly and accommodating, but honestly, I don't know how he managed it. I'm going to chalk it up to—"

He pitches his voice low so no one but Elliott can hear, barely able to keep the laughter out of his voice as he says, "Santa's magic. Always the perfect gift giver."

Elliott bursts out laughing, eyes shining bright, shoulders only shaking slightly when he pulls himself together enough to respond. "God, Nico. This is perfect. This is so, so perfect. Thank you."

MEETING A. B. IS an experience even Nico gets swept up in—he's mesmerizing to watch. He walks with poise and grace, but when he's still, he folds in on himself, shoulders slumped, posture terrible. He talks and his voice is soft and slow, but he gesticulates rapidly. He's wearing an oversized floral shirt that stops an inch or two above denim cutoffs, a pair of black fishnet tights, and scuffed black Doc Martens. Everything is a contradiction—none of it should work, and yet it does. He's charming and beautiful, and it doesn't take Nico more than their brief interaction to understand why people adore him.

Later, when they're at their seats waiting for A. B. to come on stage, Elliott slips his fingers through Nico's and squeezes. "This has been the best birthday present ever. I can't—"

He cuts himself off and turns to Nico instead of continuing. There's so much love and affection written across Elliott's face—radiating off him and into Nico— He finally gets the itch to photograph again, something Nico thought he'd never get back at this point. He wishes he had his camera with him to capture this instant forever. Although the photograph would be nothing compared to how this moment feels, it would be beautiful all the same, a constant reminder of how it looks to be loved. Standing here with Elliott watching him with so much fondness, Nico can feel the blossom of love making a home in his heart, bubbling, surging, and igniting inside. The love crests and floods through him in warm, invigorating pulses. He's so caught up in the feeling, he almost doesn't catch Elliott reiterate, "This is perfect, Nico. Thank you."

He presses a kiss against Elliott's mouth and then rests his head on his shoulder as they wait. The lights go out and then there's so much excitement coursing around him—through him—Nico's having an out-of-body experience. He squeezes Elliott's hand harder, anchoring himself to the moment, trying to block out the weight of tens of thousands of people directing their energy on one point of enjoyment, one moment of anticipation.

The emotions are so intense, they're dizzying in the same way as the amped-up experience he has when Elliott's happy—but a thousand times more magnified. The lights go off and then one spotlight shines in the middle of the stage and there A. B. is. Nico blinks and he's gone. The mood of the venue shifts into something between surprise and disappointment, but as quickly as he's gone, A. B.'s back, starting with a song Nico's not familiar with.

Elliott watches him for a moment, his focus entirely on Nico, his eyes unwavering as he gives Nico one of his slow, cheek-dimpling smiles. He's beautiful this way, surging forward and pressing a quick kiss to Nico's mouth, before turning his attention back to the stage. The noise and fire of this many emotions coming down on Nico stops abruptly. He's present again. He's here in the moment with Elliott, no longer a conduit for other people's excitement. He can actually focus on things outside their emotions. He's anchored to his own body, more in control of what he's experiencing. With his hand in Elliott's, Nico can focus again.

He takes in A. B.'s perfectly styled hair and his impeccable white jumpsuit. It's slim fitting, exceptionally well-tailored, and makes him look angelic. Nico barks out a laugh, which only gets lost in the sound of the people cheering around him, as he notices A. B. wearing the same scuffed Doc Martens from earlier. Again, it shouldn't work, but for some reason, A. B. pulls it off.

By the third song, Nico has a firm grasp on being able to tune everything out, except for the bursting happiness coming from Elliott, the vibrations of the music, and the ever-present screaming of the crowd. By the time they leave the show, it's like he's run a mile and gone shot for shot with Noelle all at the same time. He's loose and happy and carefree, and as he unlocks his door and pushes inside, Elliott trailing in behind him, it's easy for the words to start tumbling out as they head for the living room.

"So here's the thing. I love you." He has to look away from Elliott so he doesn't get distracted by his face or his mouth or the way his cheeks dimple so deep every time Nico says those three words. He runs his hand through his hair and pushes forward, because he doesn't think he's ever going to be more ready to tell Elliott everything he needs to know than he is right now. "I know it's been a while, and you've been so damn patient and haven't mentioned it once or pushed when the family stuff has come up or anything. So yeah, it's time."

Elliott's eyes widen in shock, but he smiles, softly, and encouraging, as if he knows Nico needs it. "Okay."

"Well first, I don't think I ever actually explained the hair? I know it's how the whole Santa's son revelation came to be, but yeah, it happens when you fall in love. The whole hair thing and then the beard—which I hope you like because once I'm actually Santa, and not just the heir, there's no getting rid of this thing. It'll never be shorter than it is now. So I hope you weren't attached to clean-shaven Nico."

He laughs nervously, jittery, but Elliott is a calm presence, and Nico's able to keep going. "So yeah, beard grows and comes in silver when the love is reciprocated, which brings me to the complications and obligations. Uh, yeah. So the big thing. The real kicker in the whole family tree is to come into these powers, to complete the Santafication—don't laugh—"

"I'm not laughing," Elliott says, but there is a smile tugging at his lips, and his voice is full of mirth. "It's cute is all."

Elliott's inching closer to the couch, but Nico's rooted to his spot, too wired to sit at the moment. "Anyway! The Santafication isn't complete until we're in love and loved in return. Apparently the Northern Realm—or as you'd know it, The North Pole—is some ridiculous and cheesy romantic. So yeah, none of this goes on without love. Which, go figure, I guess it makes sense if you actually think it through. But I'm getting sidetracked here. So yeah, I love you, you love me, ta-da! Santa!"

Elliott blinks: one, two, three times. He considers Nico for another long moment before asking, "Is that the complication? That you needed to fall in love? That this couldn't happen unless you were in love?"

His voice is careful and controlled and Nico purposely does not pay attention to anything other than his own nervous energy. He can't take knowing intimately how Elliott feels right now. He doesn't want to experience it before Elliott's told him.

Nico takes a deep breath and tries to answer, "Well, yeah, and then. There's uh—"

The momentum is fading, and he's having trouble getting the words out now. Elliott closes the space between them and slides his arms through Nico's. The hug is warm and tight, and as Elliott waits for an answer, he leads Nico to the couch, pushes down on his shoulders to make him sit, and then curls up next to him. The embrace and movement calm Nico enough for him to take a shaky breath and continue.

"There's a ceremony, some magical binding thing where—I don't know. I think sometimes they're at the same time and sometimes they're not, depending on when the switch is. But there's the one where I become Santa Claus when my dad retires, and all that, but then there's also the Binding—which is what they call the—I mean, listen. This is the part I've been worried to tell you. I don't want to freak you out because we've only been together for six months and only known each other a couple months longer. I know I have the very visible signs of us being in love—which has literally never happened before, by the way—but the thing is. The Santafication is only complete when the Love Fulfillment is met. Which is basically a fancy way to say we're committed to each other for life. Oh and then obviously we have to produce an heir. Which. I know we discussed adopting earlier, but I'm still—working out if it's magically conceivable in our reality because I want to do that. I want to give you that since you're being dragged into this whole mess. Let's be real, I'm sure this is not what you were expecting when you met me at Winnie's."

Elliott answers by catching Nico's mouth in a kiss. It's gentle at first, and Nico lets his walls slip for a moment, but he doesn't let them down long enough to catch anything too specific, only long enough to confirm this kiss is a sign Elliott's not freaking out. Though, Elliott deepening the kiss before pulling away with a crooked grin and eyes glinting with mischief would have been answer enough if he'd been patient. He pulls Nico up, walks them back toward Nico's room, his smile growing as they go. Elliott's hands roam Nico's body the entire time, and he punctuates each kiss—hungrier, harder, more intense—with a statement.

"So you get your powers from being in love."

Nico's hum of agreement is swallowed down by another kiss. "So without me, this isn't possible."

"Mmmhmm," Nico breathes against Elliott's mouth, and then they're kissing again. Nico's anxiety over Elliot going back through everything he's said is almost non-existent when Elliott's mouth is on his. Elliot's hands ghost over the soft skin above his waistband, and Nico has a suspicion that's exactly what Elliott wanted to accomplish.

"And it's not done until we're married."

"Well, the ceremonial part isn't but—ah—there's glowing."

It's hard to get any words out when Elliott's crowding Nico against his bedroom door, holding him there as he plants small, teasing kisses down Nico's jaw, over his neck. "Apparently. I don't know. I think my dad's full of shit—"

Nico gasps as Elliott nips at his shoulder, letting out a pleased sigh when Elliott soothes the sting with a gentle kiss. "But yeah, he said I'd know when the Santafication was done and I was fully ready to take over the post. I'll just know. That's what he said."

Elliott nods against Nico's shoulder. He reaches around him and finally pushes the bedroom door open, mouth curving in a smile as he pulls back enough to watch Nico as he leads them into Elliott's room. "Glowing, huh? Will I glow, or will you glow?"

"Oh shut up. You're teasing me."

Elliott tries to contain his smile but he's terrible at it, and even if his mouth is relatively neutral, his eyes are twinkling with the force of his giddiness. He lifts Nico's shirt off, rubs his hands up his side, and then kisses him again. This time, as he leads them backward, it's hurried and clumsy, and when the back of Nico's knees hit his bed, he's surprised to find Elliott pulling away. The whine gets caught in his throat as Elliott looks at him, and says, "And an heir."

"And an heir, yeah," Nico confirms, and he knows, he knows all too well he needs to clue him in on the timeline. He needs to tell Elliott they're nearing the end for it to all happen according to plan. But Elliott is undressing and settling between Nico's thighs to undo his jeans, and Nico can't think of anything other than this. He can deal with the rest in the morning; he's already said so much.

IN THE MORNING, he wakes up to Elliott running his fingers through the front of his hair. There's a gentle wash of affection coming from Elliott and a pulsing ball of happiness growing in Nico's chest, and he thinks there's no better way to wake up than this.

"Good morning, sunshine."

Elliott sits down next to him, nudging Nico to make room for him. "I wanted to talk to you—"

He breathes in deeply and there's a flash of nerves, but it settles in an instant, the pulsing sensation of happiness growing larger inside him. "Last night was amazing. I mean, the concert obviously. But then, after."

A bright burst of red spots Elliott's cheeks and ears and he clears his throat, but his voice still comes out a bit gruff. "We didn't really talk too much after you told me everything, and I wanted to make it clear I'm not going anywhere. You've not scared me off. I mean, I know you can tell what I'm feeling and all but—"

"It's still nice to hear it out loud," Nico says, and Elliott's responding smile is brilliant.

He throws the duvet off Nico and pulls at his arm. "Come on, I made breakfast."

Nico cocks his head to the side and raises an eyebrow, they'd been eating out this whole week. Elliott rolls his eyes. "There was pancake mix in your cabinet, but there were no eggs, so I had to improvise. They're, unfortunately, a bit dense."

"Sounds perfect," Nico says, biting down on his lip to keep from laughing.

"Shut up," Elliott says, dragging Nico out of bed. "You've been spoiling me all week. I wanted to do something nice! Not my fault you have nothing in your kitchen!"

"I haven't been here in eight months!"

Elliott places a hand on his hip and gives him a long, put-upon scowl, but then a second later, he starts laughing, conceding Nico's point. "I guess that's fair. But you can't blame me when they're terrible because I did suggest we go get a few groceries."

They sit in a comfortable silence as they eat, and the pulsing happiness in his chest, which has been there for so long, now blooms in full and washes over his entire body. It soothes the nerves rising up in his stomach and allows him to say as they're washing their dishes, "So last night—I know you said you're good with everything, and you're not going to run off but—"

He clears his throat, waiting for Elliott to dry his hands and turn back to him. He blocks out everything except for the beat of his heart and then continues, "Well, you were being quite distracting, so I didn't get to the last point, and yeah I think it's important for you to know."

Block it out. Block it out. Block it out. Elliott's eyebrows shoot up for the briefest of moments before he schools his face, but it's enough of a crack to knock all Nico's blockades down. The nerves come rushing in no matter how much Nico tries to stop them. He has to tell him now, though. He can't backtrack. "So the big kicker, the big ol' pain in my ass I've been avoiding for years is that there's a deadline to all this."

"A deadline?"

Elliott's trying not to let on what he's feeling. Nico can see he's trying, but Nico can feel Elliott's guilt building up at his inability to truly hide it, and Nico hates this. He hates this being a stipulation; he never wanted this for Elliott. He never wanted this for himself, but he especially did not want to have to bring Elliott into it. "I know it sounds intimidating... And I can't lie and say I haven't been freaking out over it for years—I've spent years not letting myself get close to anyone because I didn't—I didn't want to put this pressure on someone. I'd have preferred to give it all up, piss my dad off in the process, and leave it all behind, instead of putting this on someone I love. But then I met you. And I don't know; it seemed worth trying to put myself out there again."

"Oh, honey," Elliott says, pressing in against Nico and hugging him tight. He presses a kiss to Nico's temple and smiles against his skin, "I am so glad you took a chance with me. I—You deserve to be happy. I'm glad you thought I was worth it."

Elliott pulls back and swallows hard, and Nico closes his eyes against the onslaught of nerves coming down on him. Elliott's voice is soft and kind when he continues, and Nico forces himself to meet his eyes. "I can't imagine how nerve-wracking this has felt on your end. But, I'm glad you told me. I—we haven't talked about marriage, really, but we did discuss kids, so I've definitely been thinking of a future with you. I'm not going anywhere. This isn't freaking me out. I mean, well. There being a time frame is a little overwhelming—which you didn't say when?"

"Christmas," Nico says, throat all too tight. "Ugh. The Christmas of my thirtieth year. So yeah, this Christmas."

Elliott's hands tighten around Nico's arms, and then he's choking out, "We have to get married by this Christmas?"

Nico laughs. It's not funny but Elliott's been trying so hard to keep his emotions in check for the sake of Nico, and the sound escapes him. He cups Elliott's face in his hands and kisses him. "No, we don't have to get married by Christmas."

Elliott's face smooths out, and his shoulders relax. Nico's hit with a surge of relief before Elliott even speaks. "Okay, yeah. That would have been—that would've been too fast. I think. I'm not going anywhere, and I want to marry you one day, but this Christmas is so soon—too soon, I think. Is that okay?"

"Yeah," Nico sighs, resting his forehead against Elliott's. "It's better than okay."

Elliott's face is heating under Nico's hands, and his brow furrows. "Are you sure it's enough? Me wanting to marry you—that's plenty to—"

He flails his hands around, and Nico understands, he's asking if it will complete the Love Fulfillment, and Nico doesn't know; he doesn't feel any different, but he also doesn't care. Elliott wants to marry him one day, and it's all Nico needs to hear. "Yeah, that's enough."

THINGS DON'T CHANGE after they get back from New York, not too much. Nico goes back to the coffee shop to help but with fewer hours since things have settled some, and Elliott returns to work as the new school year begins. They continue to live together, and Nico finally calls it home. It's exactly the same as it was before but now Nico knows Elliott wants to marry him one day, and that fills him with a new level of exhilaration, one he's never experienced before, and it's the best he's ever felt, by and large.

Two weeks after they get home, he works up the courage to tell his father surrogacy is out and adoption is what he and Elliott want. He tells Kristoff they have to figure out what needs to happen to make it possible. Kristoff tries to tell Nico he doesn't know if it will work, how he's found no evidence of heirs not being biological at any point in their family history, but Nico puts his foot down, insisting he is not willing to compromise on something so important to Elliott. Kristoff concedes to doing more research and ships Nico some of the journals and books so they can split the work. It's not until a month later, when Chrysanthemum convenes with the other elves, that they discover anything substantial. The information is perfect, though, and Nico's ecstatic.

"So," Nico says over dinner, drawing the word out in a way Elliott knows means Nico wants his full attention.

Elliott puts his fork down and looks at Nico, waiting.

"So, you know how we want to adopt."

"Yes," Elliott says slowly, bristling.

Nico raises his hands, placating.

"No, no, no. Sorry. God I'm just so excited. I'm terrible at this. No, I meant my dad finally got the information we needed. We can do it. The heir doesn't have to be biological. All we have to do to make the inheritance pass to our adopted son is another ceremony. Magic loves its ceremonies, apparently."

Elliott's mouth is open in shock and Nico repeats himself, "We get to adopt a baby, Elliott."

Elliott's smile is slow, as if it's taking him a moment to process the words, but it's accompanied by an intense, heart-stuttering surge of happiness. "Oh, Nico. Thank you."

He doesn't say anything else, and Nico tries to focus on Elliott's happiness, on his beautiful, excited laughter and the way he comes over and presses his mouth against Nico's, still smiling. He tries to focus on Elliott's reaction instead of the cold sensation of disappointment falling over him. For one hopeful, fleeting moment before he told Elliott adoption was possible, he thought this would be it. He was sure this would be what pushed them over the edge of knowing, that he'd feel different, experience the glowing sensation marking the completion of the process. He hoped this would be enough.

He tries not to worry about what he'll do now, tries not to imagine what else he needs to do for Elliott to know he's ready. He tries not to think about how even though this is enough for him—Elliott's love is enough for him—there's nothing more he can do to prevent disappointing his father, letting down the family line. It's up to Elliott to get there on his own, and all he can do is wait and see.

Chapter Eighteen

IT'S SURPRISINGLY EASY for Nico to ignore, and even accept, that the deadline is fast approaching with no sign of completing the Santafication. He's had years of practice compartmentalizing this part of his life, so it doesn't bother him much after the first day, not really. He's happy with Elliott, and that's all that matters to him. If he can't be Santa because he missed some arbitrary deadline put in place centuries ago, then so be it. He doesn't care, as long as he has Elliott—he's not wanted to be Santa Claus since he knew what it entailed, anyway.

Or at least, it's how he feels until the moment he and Elliott pull up to his parents' house with Noah, Noelle, and Nadia for Thanksgiving. Then everything he put out of his mind, everything he thought he had accepted, comes crashing down on him as his father opens the door to let them in. He's standing in his childhood home and the small part of him, the part he's tried to stamp out for years now— the one wanting to please his father—grows ten times its size. He doesn't know how to get through the weekend without disappointing him in the worst way possible.

"Nico! Elliott! It is so nice to see you both!"

Before Nico has a chance to respond, Noelle pushes past them all, Nadia in her arms and an edge to her voice, "It's nice to see you, too, Dad!"

Nico dips his head in laughter and watches as Kristoff chases after her to apologize for excluding her and Noah, who chuckles from behind them and calls out, "No it's fine! I'll get the bags by myself!"

Nico grabs Elliott's hand and pulls him forward, whispering, "Welcome to hell, babe. It'll be like this all weekend."

TEMPTING FATE BY joking the weekend would be hell was apparently Nico's first mistake. He should know by now he shouldn't put things in the air that could potentially bite him in the ass. His second mistake was giving in and sitting by his father for Thanksgiving dinner. His third mistake, and the nail in his coffin, was letting his defenses down by having three glasses of wine over the course of the meal.

Except for Nadia, who Noelle is smiling down at while she rocks her to sleep, it's only the adults at the table now. The rest of the kids are playing outside with Chrysanthemum, who left the workshop in a rare turn of events to say hello to Elliott, who she'd apparently greatly missed. Kristoff is trying to get Nico's attention, but Nico can't be bothered to listen—he only has eyes for Elliott. He's sitting across from Nico, fully engrossed in conversation with Joy. Elliott had never been with Nico's entire family all at once, and Nico was impressed by how easily he slipped into the family dynamic. Everyone loved him, even Kristoff, and Nico's heart filled with a warm rush of happiness. He wanted this forever. He already knew as much, but it's especially clear now as he watches Elliott talk animatedly with his sister, eyes bright and cheeks flushed pale pink. Elliott being here makes this place feel like home in a way it hasn't since he was in college. He loves that having him here has made such a thing possible again.

"Nico darling, you seem so happy," Gloria says, and Nico reluctantly looks away from Elliott, turning to face his mom, who has taken the children leaving as an opportunity to sit next to him.

"I am," he agrees.

"Then it's happened?" Kristoff's tone is amused and conversational, but Nico immediately bristles. The time has come—he can no longer avoid this revelation, and disappointing his father is inevitable.

"No. Not yet," he says, tensing.

To Nico's surprise, Kristoff doesn't seem angry or disappointed or even too upset. His mouth turns down in a sympathetic frown, and his gaze shifts to Elliott, mouth going impossibly thin before focusing his attention back on Nico, and he wonders. He lets his walls down for a moment, focusing solely on reading his father, and he's hit with a full blast of concern. Which doesn't make sense. He should be disappointed, angry, upset Nico wasted so many years and still, at the end of it all, couldn't pull through. Instead, he's watching Nico with soft, sad eyes, and saying, "That's too bad, Nicholas. I'm truly sorry."

Gloria reaches up and brushes a strand of hair behind Nico's ear, her voice gentle and reassuring as she says, "You're almost there—it's only a matter of time."

"Yeah, I hope so," Nico says, heart aching with longing. He doesn't care if the process is complete—not past no longer disappointing his father—but he so desperately wants tangible proof Elliott is all in. It's killing him to not be sure yet if Elliott is on the same page as Nico with regards to their future.

"What are you hoping for?" Carol asks and Nico's chest aches, he seriously doesn't want to have this conversation right now.

"Oh, nothing."

Kristoff smiles and his voice is full of a proud delight Nico hasn't heard directed at him in so long. He doesn't have the heart to correct his father when he answers, "Our dear Nicholas is finally ready to take over the mantle!"

He's not. He probably never will be. All he wants is to know whether he and Elliott will last. He's not given a moment to wallow in the thought, though, because Kristoff's words bring the attention of those at the table to them. Carol and Belle squeal, and Joy exclaims with delight, "Remember when we used to play Santa, and you'd get so mad we wouldn't let you be it! Now look at you, getting your way."

Elliott watches him as his sisters and their partners react to the news, his eyes shining brightly and his smile crooked and fond—Nico's favorite.

The excitement lulls and Noelle teases, "So was there glowing? Or is Dad full of crock?"

Elliott quirks an eyebrow, and it makes Nico clam up. Then something breaks inside Nico, and he blurts out, "It's not happened yet. I don't know."

He can't take his eyes off Elliott as he speaks, can't look away as Elliott's reaction plays across his face. Elliott's voice is small when he asks, "I thought it was enough? You said—"

He doesn't finish, and Nico focuses on Elliott's emotions, and his breath catches in his throat as Elliott's pain cuts through him like a white-hot sword, piercing his heart.

Nico swallows; his chest feels tight and his throat dry. He can't form words. Noelle's standing up, hugging Nadia close to her chest, smiling gently at Nico before turning to the rest of the table and saying with an authority no one will undermine, "Okay, it's time for me to put this little one down and for the rest of you to check on your kiddos. Chrysanthemum is due for a break."

Elliott tenses as they leave, and Nico still can't look away, still can't say anything, still can't do anything but stare as his heart aches with Elliott's pain.

Once they're gone, once it's only Elliott and Nico sitting with his parents, Gloria places a gentle hand on Nico's shoulder, drawing his eyes away from Elliott, and asks finally, "What did you say was enough, Nico?"

Her voice is soft, not accusing, and Nico wants to crawl under the table. This is not how he wanted any of this to happen. He turns to Elliott again, whose eyes are wide, mouth drawn tight in a frown, and says, "It was enough for me."

Elliott's doing his best not to return Nico's attention, but when Kristoff clears his throat, Elliott flinches and his gaze snaps to Nico's. His nerves run through Nico in a surge of electricity—but not the kind they take pleasure in. It crackles too powerfully and makes Nico's skin crawl. He hates it.

"Have you talked about the future? About being together?"

Nico and Elliott answer yes at the same time, and Kristoff turns to Nico, eyes searching for something, mouth tightening slightly. "But you have not felt the change? You don't know if the Santafication is complete?"

Nico's shoulders slump, and he can hear his pulse roaring in his ears, heart pumping painfully against his ribs. "No, I haven't."

The table is silent and Gloria squeezes Nico's shoulder reassuringly as he explains, "No. You said I'd know, and I don't."

Kristoff steeples his hands in front of his face, contemplative, and Gloria suggests, "Maybe it's a time thing? Maybe they haven't been together long enough for the magic to set?"

"No," Kristoff says. "That can't be it. If the love is there, if the commitment is there—it happens. It doesn't matter how long they've been together. When I was reading through the journals for adoption information, I ran across an entry from Chip saying six weeks after he met—you know Nikolai? The one I showed you the journal of—yeah, well Chip was his dad and he completed his Santafication requirements within six weeks of meeting his wife. It's not a time thing. It just happens when it's there."

"So then..." Nico starts, shifting his gaze to Elliott. He averts his eyes as soon as Nico does, studying his hands instead.

"It would appear," Kristoff supplies. "One of you is not as committed to the other as you think."

The words hang heavy in the air, and Elliott finally locks eyes with Nico, his guilt clear as day, and Nico's heart shatters.

THE REST OF the weekend is tense and quiet between Nico and Elliott. The only thing stopping Nico from running back to his apartment in New York is the fact he came here with Noelle. They spend most of their time apart, only seeing each other at meals and when they go to sleep. Nico avoids Elliott so much he doesn't even take Elliott with him to the Northern Realm when he takes the kids, even though he knows how much he'll love it, knows how much it will mean to him. He can't imagine sharing that with him at a time like this, though, no matter how childish it may be to exclude him.

When they get back to Pine Cove, Elliott is the first to speak, his voice trembling, "I'm just scared, Nico. Worried about what it will be like to be the husband of Santa. That's— God, it's a lot to take in."

"Okay," Nico says, walking toward the bedroom.

"Okay?"

Nico stops but doesn't face him, "Yeah, okay. I understand. I don't want to be Santa Claus, so I get it. I fucking get it, okay. Doesn't mean—"

Elliott's fingers brush against Nico's wrist, and he lets himself be turned around. "I want to be ready. I want to spend my life with you, but I—"

"Don't know if you want to spend your life with Santa Claus," Nico finishes and Elliott nods.

Nico laughs, a bitter burst of air, and Elliott scrunches his nose, an action Nico would find utterly endearing under any other circumstance. "Well, babe, if you don't want to spend your life with Santa then we don't have to worry. It's not going to happen!"

Elliott's eyes narrow, fingers tightening around his wrist. "Nico—"

"Shh, okay? Shh," Nico says, his voice coming out far gentler than he expected as a sense of peace washes over him. "I love you and I'm not— What am I going to do? Go find someone in a month? No! I want you! You want me. I've never wanted—I have *never* pictured a future with anyone. God, not even Taylor and I was young and caught up in being away from home, and I thought he was the one! And even still! Nothing. You know that! I've told you that. You're it for me! You know this is the first time I have ever planned for the future with someone, that I've ever let myself imagine being happier for longer than the here and now. We don't—it doesn't have to be complicated. It doesn't have to be some magic-inducing, world-changing bullshit. I don't care about any of it. I care about you. It's enough for me. It's always been enough for me."

"I—" Elliott starts, snapping his mouth shut. Nico knows Elliott's emotions are all over the place. His stomach is roiling with the conflict Elliott is experiencing, and he's relieved when Elliott presses a kiss against the corner of his mouth, and sighs. "Yeah, okay."

Chapter Nineteen

NICO FULLY BELIEVES it is okay until Elliott proposes on his birthday. For an instant, Nico's whole body vibrates with happiness, but then the illusion is shattered. It feels so good to share happiness in these moments, to feel Elliott's mingle with his own, so he lets his walls down for the first time in weeks and *feels*. He expects to be swept away by it. Expects a dizzy rush of excitement, happiness that amplifies and multiplies inside him. Instead, there's a sizzling of nerves over his skin and a gush of guilt in the pit of his stomach.

This isn't right. This isn't how it's supposed to be. There should be glowing, or *something,* to let him know the process is complete. At the very least, he should feel his own happiness at the prospect of marriage reflected through Elliott's emotions. Instead, he's fizzing out, deflating.

"No," Nico says, and while Elliott's face falls, his emotions betray the reality he's trying to conceal. Nico can feel the relief washing over him, gentle and calming in a way it should be, but it makes bile rise in Nico's throat. His heart is breaking, and he's moments away from throwing up or screaming.

"No," Elliott repeats, shocked. After Elliott's relief fades, Nico can tell the tone of Elliott's voice is the truth. The surprise jolts through him, setting his nerves alight, and the fact Elliott expected him to say yes when his heart wasn't in it, when he had to know he'd feel it, makes it so much worse.

"Did you think I wouldn't know?"

Elliott at least has the dignity to look ashamed. He may even feel it, but Nico can't tell at the moment; all he feels is numb. Elliott peers at his shoes and mumbles unintelligibly and then straightens up, meeting Nico's gaze head-on. He shrugs. His voice is strong and determined, "I thought it was the right thing to do. That it's what I should do. I love you."

He reaches for Nico's hand, and Nico pulls away, and the way Elliott's face falls makes a sick, twisted satisfaction boil inside Nico. This isn't right. This is not how Nico imagined this happening. This is not how he wanted any of this to be.

"I'm not going to marry you if you only think it's what you *should* do and not what you w*ant* to do."

Nico's surprised by how calm he sounds when his body has moved past numb and started ripping in two. It builds up and then whites out and all Nico feels is a dull, painful ache in the middle of his chest.

Elliott's face goes tight and Nico's vaguely aware of his fear, his guilt, his embarrassment, his shame. *Yep, he was ashamed.* It all passes through Nico as if it's happening to someone else, as if it's a ghost of a feeling Nico can't quite register within himself. Nico can't *feel* them, not how he's supposed to be able to.

"I love you, Nico. I do. You know I do!" He sounds panicked, and Nico breaks.

Tears well up in Nico's eyes, and he tries so hard not to let Elliott see how much he's hurt him. He swallows hard around the lump in his throat and tries to keep his voice even. "I do, but this—"

His voice breaks as he gestures to Elliott's hand. He's still holding the stupid prize ring he got off one of the cupcakes from the celebration earlier. Elliott's hand flinches as Nico motions for it, his palm closing around the plastic, and Nico snaps, "This is wrong. This isn't what I wanted.

This isn't how it's supposed to be. Goddammit, Elliot! Was I not perfectly fucking clear my happiness with you is more important than this stupid fucking family obligation? I told you I didn't care if it didn't happen in time! I told you that!"

"I know! I know you did. But I thought— Shit! I saw this stupid ring on the fucking cupcakes, and I thought about it. I pictured how I would propose to you, in the future. And it made me so happy I thought I could be ready. I thought if I asked you, if I proposed now, it'd be enough. That it would seal the thing, that it would complete this thing for you. I thou— I hoped it wouldn't matter I didn't want—that I wasn't ready right this moment to be Santa's husband because I *do* want to marry you. I want to marry you so much. I want to adopt a child with you. I want to stand next to you while you do all of this. I do. I want all of this with you. I just..."

He trails off and Nico takes a moment to concentrate on feeling. It's still distant but he can make out the warm sincerity of Elliott's words building up inside him, trying to claw their way out of Nico's numbness, but they don't catch. Nico doesn't let them. Even so, Nico can make out a glimmer of apprehension under all the sincerity and it must be the only part that matters to the universe.

Nico closes his eyes and tries to keep his voice steady. "I can feel you mean what you're saying. I know you're telling the truth. But there's something holding you back because if there wasn't—we'd know! I'd know! This would be over, and we wouldn't have to worry about it again until my father retired. But that's *not happening.*"

Elliott stands there, dumbstruck, not saying anything, and Nico knows he has to leave. He can't be here right now. There're too many emotions trying to claw their way into making him *feel* something, but all he's really processing is how everything's falling apart.

"I'm going to go stay with Noelle."

Pain. Shame. Fear. They're all fighting to take over, but Nico won't let them. He doesn't want to know what Elliott is feeling. He doesn't want to care, and yet he still attempts to soothe Elliott. "I know you wanted to do right by me, that you thought this would make me happy. And in a way, I can appreciate what you did, but I need—"

The tears fall, he can't do anything to stop them now. Elliott's there, wrapping his arms around his shoulders, and Nico sinks into him, let's himself be tugged closer and soothed by Elliott's warm embrace. He's sobbing, and his throat is tight, and his eyes are burning, and Elliott squeezes him harder, whispers a litany of "Sorry" into his hair. Nico wants nothing more than to rewind time and make it to where he never has to feel this way again.

He doesn't know how long they stay there embracing, but when he pulls away, Elliott's shirt is wet with Nico's tears, and Nico's throat is dry and aching. He wipes at his eyes and Elliott says, firmly and sincerely, "I am so sorry, Nico. I should never have tried to force the magic to happen. It was a dumb, rash decision. I wanted to give this to you, to help you to not have to wait, and I am so sorry I've hurt you."

"I need some time," Nico says. He grabs his keys from the counter and shrugs, gaze darting everywhere but to Elliott. "I know you're sorry."

His laugh is bitter and mean as he waves his hand over his body. "That's what got us into this, y'know. I can feel every goddamn thing you do. You could have never pulled this one off, Elliott! And I think that's what hurts the most. You knew deep down there was no way I was going to *feel* this as sincere, and you did it anyway. *On my goddamn birthday!* Oh, happy thirtieth birthday, babe! Do you want me to rip your heart out before or after cake?"

"Nico, please. Please, let's talk some more. I don't want you to leave like this. I—you— I'm so sorry."

Elliott's voice is a broken, jagged plea, and Nico almost, almost loses his will to go. But he needs to do this; he needs to step back and see how he feels in the morning. He needs to assess his emotions when Elliott's aren't mixing with his own, when he can make sure he cares for Elliott the same way he did before his spontaneous proposal.

He forces himself to meet Elliott's eyes. "I need some time. I need you to give me some time, okay?"

Elliott nods and Nico turns on his heel to leave. He doesn't say anything until Nico has one foot out the door, and even then, it's so quiet Nico's not even sure he's meant to hear. But the words ring in his ear as loudly as if Elliott shouted them right next to him. "Please know I never meant to hurt you."

Nico pauses, hand tightening around the doorknob. He sighs, steadies his voice and says, "I know," as he shuts the door. He's not sure if Elliott hears him, but it doesn't matter—he lets him leave, and it's the best thing he's done for Nico all day.

ELLIOTT GIVES HIM plenty of time and space, and with each passing day, the icy numbness that's taken Nico over since his birthday thaws a little bit more. Elliott doesn't call or come by the coffee shop when Nico's working, but a week after the failed proposal, he sends a text with only a clock emoji and a question mark right as Nico's shift is ending. It makes him laugh, the ice in his heart melting even more. He doesn't respond, though.

Once he caves and tells Noelle what transpired between the two of them, he comes to a conclusion that completely melts the ice and warms his heart again. He calls Elliott four days after the initial message, and while he knows he'll be in school, Nico still sighs in relief when it goes to voicemail. He needs to be able to say this without Elliott interjecting; it's important he gets this out in one go.

"Elliott, I've missed you and I love you. I needed to say that first because I think the rest will be hard for you to swallow, but I think in the end it's what's right for us—what will rectify the situation. I've talked it through with Noelle, and I th— No, I know I need to go home to New York. I need to spend some time away from my family and just be me. I've had the time of my life with you this year, and it made me forget for a moment how little joy I've had for the holidays the last few years. Being with you filled me with so much happiness I forgot, even a little, how much I've been dreading this deadline for *years*. As soon as I was old enough to understand the implications of the deadline— there was literally a clock ticking down telling me to fall in love or else—I've hated it. It took all the wonder out of being Santa Claus—something I always used to want. It made me feel I had no control over my own life even though they're all my feelings. What we feel—this thing between us? It's the realest thing I've ever had, and that's why I know I need to let the clock run out. I never wanted to tell you there was a deadline and make you feel pressured to *make it happen*. And that's exactly what happened. I didn't want you to feel this way, the way I've felt for so long, walking around like you have no control over how things are going, like your hands are being forced by the powers that be. I want this to be out of our heads and off our backs, so I'm letting the time run out. Which is my decision. This is my family and my obligation, and I know you wanted to help, and I appreciate it, I do, but this is what I want. I love you, and I miss you, and I will talk to you after Christmas when this is over, and we can just be. Have a good Christmas, Elliott."

He turns his phone off the moment he hangs up and heads for New York. He's at peace with his decision, relieved he's finally taking his life into his own hands. Noelle knows what he's doing and supports him entirely. With that in mind, knowing someone knows where he is and can find him if something important happens, he lets himself check out and worry about nothing but himself. He needs to focus on himself and not get wrapped up in what he's supposed to do for his family like he has all these years. This is what he wants. This is what he's probably always wanted. To not have the fate of his love life tied so deeply with magic he never signed up for and a clock ticking down he never wanted to be aware of.

When he gets home, it's nice to sit in his apartment and not do anything, not even having to put on his best face in front of his family for the holidays. It's nice to sit on his couch and know soon he'll never have to worry about fulfilling this ever again—it will be out of his hands. It will be over.

AS THE CLOCK ticks down on Christmas, Nico's heart starts to race. This is what he wants, he knows he does, but wanting it and following through with it have always been different things. He wants to be free of this feeling, of not having control of his own life. He wants to know he's made this decision for himself and it wasn't thrust upon him by someone else. As the clock strikes twelve, and the Christmas of his thirtieth year ends, Nico's heartbeat steadies, and his whole body relaxes with relief. He's finally put himself first, and it feels magnificent. It finally feels right.

A moment later, there's a knock on his door. For a second, he thinks it must be his father coming to rip him a new one for ruining the family line, but he knows if Kristoff intended to do so it would have happened days ago. He opens the door and Elliott's there, smiling back at him like Nico's the best thing he's ever seen.

"Hey," he says, and Nico feels like the breath has been punched out of him.

"Hey," Nico breathes out, and Elliott's smile grows impossibly wide as Nico swings the door all the way open, gesturing for him to come in.

"I missed you," they say at the same time, and then they're laughing. Elliott reaches out first, fingers curling gently against Nico's hips, and then they're kissing. It's been so long, too long, and Nico is vibrating with happiness. It starts in his heart and radiates out, coursing through his veins, igniting his nerves. The love he feels, the love Elliott feels, blooms and blooms and blooms until there's no more room for the emotion to grow. When the sensation settles over him—warm and comfortable and right—Nico knows.

"Holy shit," Nico says, laughing as he pulls away from Elliott's mouth. He makes a disappointed sound at the back of his throat and pouts back at Nico.

"It's done," Nico says, awestruck.

Elliott's brow furrows in confusion, and Nico doesn't understand either, but he *knows*. "The process. The Santafication. It's done. I can feel it. It's done. I'm—I'm eligible to be Santa?"

To Nico's utter surprise Elliott's mouth curls up, smile growing with each passing second, and Nico's hit with a wave of dizzying happiness.

"You're happy," he says dumbly.

"I am," Elliott agrees.

"I thought you didn't—this means when my dad retires I can take over. I thought you weren't ready for that. I thought you were still apprehensive over being Santa's— about being my husband."

Elliott bites his lip, eyes never leaving Nico's. "When you left your voicemail, I was so— I felt so much. I wanted to go to you immediately and tell you not to ruin your family's legacy for me. That didn't feel right. But then I— Well, I already tried to take matters into my own hands, and we saw how that turned out. I tried to ask you to marry me out of misguided obligation, and it wasn't right. This had to be your decision. If giving it all up was what you wanted, then I wanted to be there for you when you got back. And then I realized none of the other stuff matters. I was being— I don't know—a worrywart. I was getting in my own head. I want you. I want this. I'm ready to move forward with you if you'll have me back."

Nico's smiling, cupping Elliott's face in his hands, teasing, "What happened to waiting for me to come back? You're here."

Elliott's eyes twinkle with laughter. "But not until after Christmas—until it was the twenty-sixth. I've been pacing outside your door for the last half hour."

"Of course, you have," Nico says and Elliott shrugs.

His cheeks flush bright pink, but his voice is firm and confident as he speaks, "You know I'm impatient when it comes to you."

"Thank you for waiting. Thank you for not knocking until the deadline passed. I'm glad I did it. I don't know. It's made my resentment for the whole thing mellow out a bit, knowing even though we didn't make it happen before Christmas, the Santa line wasn't going to die out. Kind of seems like I had more control of it even though I'm still eligible. Like it happened despite my defiance, not because I played into the game. Maybe it's dumb but—"

Elliott cuts him off, and Nico feels impossibly warm when he says, with firm conviction, "It's not dumb."

Nico is pleased by the affirmation, but he has one more thing to ask before he can get swept up by all this. "Of course I'll take you back— I never— You never lost me. But I need to know first—have your feelings toward being Santa's husband changed? I mean, I think they must have, because we're standing here, and I know, but I need to hear you say it."

Elliott doesn't answer for a moment, and Nico concentrates on the feel of his skin under his hands, the pink of his lips, the green of his eyes, anything but the emotions he could be experiencing. He wants to be surprised by Elliott's words.

"They have," Elliott says, and Nico's breath catches; hearing it out loud is better than he imagined. "When you were willing to disregard all your family obligations so there wouldn't be any pressure on our relationship, I realized it didn't matter if this was a lot to handle. I wanted to be with you—no matter what. By your side for everything. Always. And if that meant you being Santa Claus and me being his husband, then that's what I wanted. I thought I had realized too late, but I guess not."

Nico surges forward and kisses Elliott. It's slow and gentle, and it feels like a promise. Nico still has his reservations about being Santa, about becoming the icon, but with Elliott by his side, and the knowledge he forged his own fate—that he took centuries of Hamurişi family legend and turned it on its head and carved his own path—Nico can face anything.

Epilogue

IT'S BEEN ALMOST three entire years since time ran out on Nico's countdown. Letting the deadline pass was the biggest decision he ever made, and it only felt right for him and Elliott to have their Binding on the anniversary of the Santafication being completed, despite their Love Fulfillment occurring after the given timeline. At the time, Nico believed nothing would ever top the moment Elliott knocked on his door and kissed him on the twenty-sixth. It was the moment he knew he fulfilled his destiny, but even that doesn't hold a candle to this one.

He and Elliott are standing in front of the Great Flake waiting for midnight to pass and their Binding Ceremony to begin and Nico doesn't think his heart's beat this fast. Ever. It's hammering against his ribs, the sound pulsing in his ears; it's heating his entire body with anticipation. The only thing keeping him grounded in the moment, keeping his mind steady and focused, is Elliott's hand in his as they wait for Christmas to end once again.

While all Bindings happen outside of the earthly wedding, it's not out of the ordinary for them to happen on separate instances— he and Elliott will get married in Pine Cove next Saturday. What *is* unusual is for a Binding to happen without Chrysanthemum officiating. She's been at every one of the proceedings since the very first, but Nico insisted this time it only be him and Elliott. She'd told them what the ceremony entailed, exactly what to do and when to do it, but refused to give them her blessing to go alone until they could recite her directions back verbatim.

"Three, two, one," Elliott says, pulling his hand away from Nico's as the Great Flake's pulsing blue light grows in intensity. "It's time, Nico."

Nico nods, following Elliott as he steps right up to the Great Flake. They place their hands on the light in unison and push, waiting.

The light throbs under their hands, growing brighter and brighter with each pulse, and soon there's a chilling sensation coursing through his hand. Elliott sucks in a breath beside him and Nico knows he feels it too.

They step back as the blue light turns gold and then fades to its usual brightness, once again blue. Nico and Elliott turn their bodies to each other but keep their attention settled on the Great Flake before them. They clasp their outstretched right hands together and watch as soft tendrils of blue light come from the center of the Flake, wrapping around their held hands.

"I love you," Nico says first.

The light pulses, and there's a rush of warmth around their hands, and Elliott gives him a watery smile, his voice choked as he says, "I love you too."

The tendrils of light twist farther up their arms, blue light turning golden as it snakes its way up their shoulders and across their chests. Nico watches in astonishment as the light disappears into Elliott's chest, making him glow with the same beautiful, golden light previously around his arm.

Elliott's still got tears in his eyes, but they're widening in shock, eyebrows shooting up as he laughs, "And you'd given up on the glowing—look at you!"

Nico's laughing, too, but he can't take his eyes off Elliott. "I'll have to take your word for it. Don't want to look at anything but you."

"Am I glowing, too?" he asks, but he doesn't check for himself.

"Yeah," Nico says, breath hitching as Elliott's smile grows. "And you're beautiful."

"I'll have to take your word for it," Elliott repeats, a teasing grin transforming his face. "I seem to only have eyes for you."

Nico's not sure how long they stand there staring at each other. He remembers Chrysanthemum saying the ceremony is actually quite brief, but it feels so much longer. It's like time has stopped, and the world has stilled for him and Elliott to have this moment together. It seems an eternity before the light leaves Elliott's body and starts slithering back down his arm. Nico watches as the tendrils of light around their joined hands grow brighter. This time, the beautiful golden glow increases until it's too bright, and Nico has to close his eyes to shield them from the intensity.

When he opens his eyes a beat later, he has to blink away the spots before he can focus on the change that's occurred. Elliott's smiling, touching his left hand to his mouth in a gesture of quiet surprise, and Nico's sees it: a glint of light on his ring finger. He steps forward and pulls Elliott's hand away from his mouth, taking it in both hands to get a better look. And there it is, on his left ring finger, a thin ice-white band like the ones his parents have. He rubs his thumb over the surface of the ring, cold to touch—but not unpleasant—and identical to the surface of the Great Flake. The ceremony is complete, the Great Flake has Bound them, forged their rings from the depths of its magic and joined them for the rest of their lives.

"Well, Elliott," Nico says after a moment, voice coming out every bit as awestruck as he feels. "How's it feel to be the husband of the very next Santa Claus?"

Elliott's smile is brighter than any of the light the Great Flake surrounded them with. "It feels magical, Nico. Just like you."

Acknowledgements

First, I'd like to thank my husband Kenny who, despite being absolutely useless at helping name characters, was immeasurably encouraging throughout this whole journey. Second, a gigantic thank you to Kim(othy) for dragging me kicking and screaming away from distractions and keeping me on track. Never once letting me give up on this book—no matter how sure I was I'd never finish.

To everyone who saw my annual live-tweets lamenting the lack of queer holiday romcoms and replied saying they'd read my story when it was nothing more than a concept about "Santa's gay son," this book would not be possible without that encouragement. To anyone who ever answered one of my Twitter polls during the planning of this book, whether the results corresponded to what I wanted or not, you always helped me decide what I thought was best for the story.

And finally, to Barb: thank you for working with me to make *Love Blooms* the best it could be.

About the Author

Thematically, Stephanie enjoys magic and spies and magical spies. Aesthetically, she loves glitter and gold and pineapples. She wants to put more soft, sweet bi representation into the world so those similar to her teen-self can see themselves in their favorite genres and know who they are is nothing to be ashamed of.

She currently lives in the Great White North (Wisconsin) with her husband, daughter, and three dogs. The only thing getting her through these Midwest winters is the soothing sound of Tim Riggins saying "Texas forever" and the prospect of one day moving back there.

She loves a good astrology Twitter account but ultimately only believes in it when her husband calls her stubborn, and then her response is: "Well, I am a Taurus."

Twitter: @glitterhoyt

Website: www.stephanieahoyt.com

Other books by this author

A Holiday Ruse

Also Available from NineStar Press

Connect with NineStar Press

Website: NineStarPress.com

Facebook: NineStarPress

Facebook Reader Group: NineStarNiche

Twitter: @ninestarpress

Tumblr: NineStarPress